The Long Journey

Barbara Corcoran

The Long Journey

illustrated by Charles Robinson

Atheneum 1972 *New York*

To Bradford Angier

"Black Rook in Rainy Weather," from *The Colossus*.
Copyright © 1960 by Sylvia Plath.
Reprinted with permission of Olwyn Hughes.

Copyright © 1970 by Barbara Corcoran
All rights reserved
Library of Congress catalog card number 79-115067
Published simultaneously in Canada
by McClelland & Stewart Ltd.
Manufactured in the United States of America
by Halliday Lithograph Corporation
West Hanover, Massachusetts
Designed by Harriett Barton
First Printing July 1970
Second Printing June 1971
Third Printing February 1972

The Long Journey

chapter 1

Laurie reined in her horse at the place where the hill dropped away. She sat quietly for a moment looking down at the ghost town that was her home. Beside her ran narrow rails that had once carried little cars full of ore from the mine to the mill below. The hillside had eroded and the rails, rusted and twisted, hung down in space. The mill had boards missing in its sides, and its roof had caved in.

Off to the right on another hillside were a dozen little shacks where the miners had lived, and to the left was the long building they had used for a dining and recreation hall. Everything now was empty, falling apart, except the little house where she and her grandfather lived, and the mine itself where he still poked around in bone-chilling depths looking for gold. Once this had been one of the greatest gold-producing mines in Montana, but that was years ago. Years and years ago.

She watched her grandfather make his way slowly up the hill, far below her, toward their cabin. He used a cane that he had made out of a mountain ash limb, and he poked ahead of himself with it as he walked. He was getting worse. Something was going to have to be done.

She turned her horse's head and started back down the other side of the hill. "Come on, Hook," she said, "we'd better get on home." Hook was half Hambletonian, half quarter horse. Her grandfather had won him in a poker game on one of his rare visits to town three years before. Hook had been a colt then, and Laurie had named him after the white blaze on his forehead that was shaped like a fishhook. With his Hambletonian heritage he could trot faster than most horses could gallop. Laurie was very proud of him.

Hook picked his way carefully down the steep hill, and they rode along what had once been the main street of the little town. There there were small one-story buildings that still had their signs, faded now almost to illegibility. Assayer's office, sheriff's office, bar, barbershop. Laurie had often played in them, pretending that people still occupied them. She liked to sit in the barber's chair and stare at her image in the cloudy mirror or sit on one of the bar stools and pretend that she was a miner with a sackful of gold.

Ten of her thirteen years had been spent here with her grandfather. Her parents had been killed in an automobile accident when she was three and she had no other family except a bachelor uncle in Butte. Her grandfather had kept her presence as quiet as possible because he was afraid the authorities would take her away from him.

"Institutions," he said over and over. "You got to watch out for 'em, or people will clap you in some doggone hole. All people can think about is institutions. Schools, hospitals, welfare societies, orphan asylums, old folks' homes, poor farms . . . That's all they can think of. They're like sheep. What we got to do is keep you here till you're big enough to stand up in the world and defend yourself against 'em, without somebody clapping you into some doggone institution."

The one that really frightened her was the orphan asylum. Her grandfather had told her dreadful tales of little girls in black uniforms marching two by two, not allowed to speak or play. He said he had seen an orphan asylum once and that was how it was.

So she lived her life in and around the ghost town, playing her own games, inventing her own companions. Sometimes she played with some Indian children who lived a few miles away, but she had never known white children. Her grandfather was a good companion, always ready to take her fishing or hunting with him or to play checkers with her or just talk. He had a store of wonderful stories about his life, and many about the Saturday Mine, the mine in this little town that had been called Hawkins Dry Diggings.

He had come to the Saturday Mine when it was almost played out, but he had made quite a pile of money from it just the same; and in the end he had bought the whole place. The money was gone now, but he was still able to dig out enough gold by hand to keep them in groceries.

In the summer they had a vegetable garden and in the fall he always got a deer or an elk. He had great faith in the Saturday Mine. He was sure it had a lot of gold in there yet and he talked constantly of raising enough money to operate it properly.

"There's a fortune in there," he often told her. "Don't you ever let go of that mine if anything happens to me."

Now something was happening to him. He was going blind. It had come on gradually, first in the left eye and now in the right. At first he had not mentioned it. Then one day when he had crashed into a table and fallen, he told her.

"I know it can be fixed," he said, "but I'm not going to any hospital. No institutions for Peter Bent. They get you in there and they won't let you out."

But the loss of eyesight had grown worse, and now he had to move very carefully to avoid falling. Laurie was worried. She had begged him to let her go for a doctor.

Finally he had admitted that perhaps he did need help. "But I got to study it," he said. "I got to see what's the best thing to do."

She let Hook carry her down the weed-choked road. It was July, and the air was full of white flying cotton from the cottonwood trees. Beyond their own hill the mountains rose up in jagged peaks, still streaked with snow. The sun was hot. It was a good time of year. Summer made her feel free after the snowbound winter.

During the winter there was not much to do. She skied and snowshoed and sometimes skated if the river was clear of snow. And she read and re-read the boxes of books that had belonged to her parents. Her father had been a high school English teacher.

When she was old enough for school, her grandfather enrolled her for correspondence courses, the kind the state had set up for children who lived too far from any school. She liked the lessons, and she was always way ahead of where she was supposed to be. One of her teachers last year had written to her several times and finally had said she would like to come visit her. Laurie had been delighted, but her grandfather had been alarmed.

"She just wants to check up on you," he said. "She'll tell the authorities it ain't fit for you to be living way out here with just me, and they'll take you away."

Laurie was sure he was wrong; Miss Bickford had sounded so nice in her letters. But when it was time for Miss Bickford to come—for there had not been time to tell her not to—Laurie had obediently hidden in the old building where the miners used to eat. She had scraped away a patch of dirt from one of the windows and watched Miss Bickford come up the bumpy road in a little green car that looked like a sow bug. Laurie had watched her get out and look around uncertainly, a white-haired lady who looked nice.

Grandfather came out of the cabin and took off his hat and talked to her, and pretty soon she rode away again. It had made Laurie feel terribly lonesome to see her go. She had felt like crying. She had never thought of Hawkins Dry Diggings as lonely before.

Afterward Grandfather had told her that he had said she was in Butte visiting her Uncle Arthur.

"But that was a lie," Laurie said. She was shocked. He had always said it was wrong to lie.

"I know it," he said, "and I don't feel good about it.

But I didn't know what to do. The woman had me trapped." He looked upset. "She said you're a very smart girl."

The next week he told her he had subscribed to the *National Geographic* for her. The arrival of the *Geographic* became one of the best times of the month. She read every word.

She knew a good deal about the pygmies of Africa, the aborigines of Australia, far places in Asia, but she had never seen a city. She knew the routes that planes and ships took to go around the world, but she had never heard the whistle of a train. It was a lopsided way to grow up, and she knew it; but she also knew that it was better than any orphan asylum. Some day she would travel all over the world and see everything.

"It ain't all it's cracked up to be," her grandfather told her. "It's full of folks fighting and being mean to each other. Riots, wars, starvation, folks too poor, folks too rich. It's no great shakes of a world."

But she wanted to see it just the same.

Hot and dusty, she slid down off Hook's bare back and turned him into the corral. She would just check on her grandfather, and if he was all right, she would take a shower before she began to fix supper. Her grandfather had always done the cooking but now it was hard for him. Laurie was still inexpert but she did her best.

She went to the door of the cabin and looked in. It was a small three-room cabin with two bedrooms, the kitchen an extension of the living room.

Her grandfather was lying on the sofa with his eyes closed. Not sure whether he was asleep or not, she waited a moment but he didn't move so she went on out to the shower house, a little wooden lean-to just big enough for one person to stand up in. A bucket of water hung on a spike above her head. Laurie took off her clothes, stood under the bucket and pulled the attached rope. The bucket tilted and a shower of cold water splashed down on her. It made her shiver but it felt good. She soaped herself vigorously, tilted the bucket again and then stepped out of the shower gasping and glowing. She rubbed herself hard with the towel that hung on a nail. She would have to go down to the river after a while and refill the shower bucket. Her grandfather wouldn't let her carry it, though. After she filled it, he brought it up the hill.

She rubbed her hair with the towel. Her grandfather had always cut her hair for her. Now it was long and shaggy. She had tried cutting it herself, but the results had been disastrous. There were still ragged places where she had hacked at it.

After she had dressed, she got some water for Hook and then went back into the cabin. Her grandfather was sitting at the table with his head on his hands. The thing that frightened her most about his condition was the attacks of depression that overcame him. He had always taught her that you could lick anything if you tried hard enough, and she had believed him. Now she saw him struck down by something he couldn't lick.

He lifted his head when she came into the cabin.

"How are you feeling, Grandpa?" she said.

"Everything is all right," he said. He was trying to sound like his old cheerful self, but it didn't ring true.

"What would you like for supper?"

"Well, we've still got those rabbits. How about fried rabbit?"

"All right." Lately she had done a little hunting on her

own, to keep them going. She didn't like killing animals, but they had to eat. "Would you like hush puppies too?" He had taught her how to mix up cornmeal and flour and onion to make hush puppies.

"Whatever you want," he said, which was not like him. He usually had definite ideas about meals.

She went out to the well and pulled on the rope that held the little wooden platform where they kept their perishable food. She felt the cool dampness of the well as she reached her arms in and got the dressed rabbits. She took out some butter, too. They had a cow named Gertrude, who kept them supplied with milk and butter. Her grandfather was still able to milk the cow. She was not sure what would happen when he no longer could. She had tried it and it had gone very badly, with Gertrude kicking over the milk pail and hitting Laurie in the face with her tail.

She cooked the rabbits and the hush puppies, and the two ate in an unaccustomed silence. Laurie could see that her grandfather was thinking, and she did not want to interrupt him.

After dinner was over and the dishes washed up, he said, "We've got to have us a little talk, Laurie."

It always alarmed her when he took that serious tone. She had never gotten over the fear that some day he might decide she was too much trouble for him.

"Well," he said, after a long pause, "I guess we got to do something."

She looked at him. He was a tall thin man with white hair and a tanned clean-shaven face. He was sixty-three and except for the trouble with his eyes, he was very healthy. It hurt her to see him fumble about and move cautiously, he who had always strode with long purposeful steps anywhere he chose.

"I've been thinking about it for some time," he said. He looked at her, narrowing his eyes in an effort to focus on her. "The only thing I can think of is for you to go to Arthur."

Laurie's chest tightened. "You mean to stay?"

"No, no. To get help."

"Couldn't I get the doctor in town?" she said.

He slapped his hand on the table. "No, sir. Miller is a good man, but the first thing he'd do would be to clap me in the hospital. I know how it goes. I'd get in there, and I'd stay there till I died. I'm not having any of that. Arthur understands me. He'd make sure no doctor did anything like that to me, and he'd make sure nobody carted you off to any orphanage either. Arthur's a good boy."

Her Uncle Arthur came up about once a year to go on a hunting trip. He was a big, hearty, kind man.

"We can trust Arthur," her grandfather went on. "Don't know anybody else I'd trust."

"But he lives in Butte," she said.

"That's right. And Butte is clear at the other end of the state. But I don't see any other way around it. You and Hook have got to go get Arthur."

chapter 2

Laurie was both frightened and excited at the idea of going to Butte. It would be a tremendous adventure, and she always longed for adventures. But who knew what would happen?

"You could go part of the way by bus," her grandfather said, "but I don't want you doing that. The authorities would pick you up first thing, a young girl your age riding the bus alone."

"Won't they pick me up anyway?" she said.

"Not if you stay out of their way. Stay out of towns as much as you can. Keep in the country. You know your way in the country—you know how to live off the land. You and Hook can make it."

"Maybe I could telephone Uncle Arthur," Laurie said.

"No, no," he said impatiently. "Telephones are no good. Can't half the time hear what the other fellow is saying. You'd never be able to explain everything like it's got to be explained. No, there's nothing to do but go there." He sighed. "I hate to send you on such a long journey and you so young."

"Well," she said, "you did worse things than that when you were my age, and younger."

He brightened up a little. "That's right, I sure did. I went to work when I was nine years old. Used to light the street lamps."

Laurie smiled. She had heard his stories many times but she always enjoyed them and now especially she wanted to get his mind off the present.

"I tell you, it was a cold job in winter. That old wind would come whistling along and blow out the flame as fast as I lit it. We had gas lamps then, you know. I like to froze, some nights."

"Tell about when you drove the lumber wagon," she said.

"I was a big boy, then. Fourteen. I used to drive this long wagon loaded with logs. Had two mules to pull it. And I drove it through the mountains. The road was just wide enough to let us through. And it dropped off a thousand feet or more. Lots of hairpin turns and switchbacks. I got good money for that job because nobody else would take it."

"I ain't ever had anything exciting like that happen to me," Laurie said.

He wagged his finger at her. "Don't say 'ain't'."

"You say it sometimes," she said. They went through

this conversation often.

"I'm a tough old man. I say lots of things I shouldn't. But I know better. Don't forget, I went back to high school when I was nineteen years old because I wanted to marry your grandmother. I didn't want to disgrace her, her being a schoolteacher. I got my diploma when I was twenty-one. I had to take a lot of guff from those kids but I stuck it out. And you're going to high school as soon as I can see my way clear. And you aren't going to say 'ain't'."

"All right, I won't," she said.

He was silent for a minute. "I wish I'd had your grandmother here to help me bring you up after we lost your mama and father," he said sadly. "Your grandmother was a real lady, Laurie."

"I know it," Laurie said. "I can tell by her picture."

"I don't know if I did right, leaving her alone so much, but I had the gold fever. She died of the pneumonia when I was away in the hills. I'll never get over that. Died all alone in a damned hospital." Then he sat up straight. "Well, what's done is done. Now you get down that fishing tackle box that's up there in the cupboard."

Laurie got the box and put it on the table. Her grandfather's hands fumbled a moment for the catch and then snapped the box open. There were papers inside. He took them out, holding them up close to his eyes. He felt of them carefully and finally picked out one. "You look at that and see if it doesn't say 'deed of property'."

"Yes, it does," she said.

"All right. Now I want you to carry that with you everywhere you go. Don't let anybody take it away from you."

"What is it?" Laurie asked.

"It's a deed I had made out some years ago, making this property over to you and me, joint. You're half owner of this whole place, the mine and the town and all. And if anything was to happen to me, it'd be all yours."

Laurie was impressed. "I didn't know you'd done that," she said. It made her feel grown-up.

"You're a property owner. If anybody tries to bother you, just show them that paper. As long as you're a property owner, you got certain rights. And if anything happens to me, I want you to promise you'll hang onto this mine, and as soon as you see your way clear, you work it. Get Arthur to advise you. I tell you, Laurie, there's a fortune in that mine. If I just had the capital . . ." He sighed. "Anyway you're half owner of the Saturday Mine."

"That's nice," she said.

He took out of the box something wrapped in a blue gingham handkerchief, opened up the corners of the handkerchief and took out a little soft leather pouch with a drawstring. He opened the pouch and dumped out the contents. There were three large gold nuggets. "You take these with you," he said. "Don't let them go if you can help it. I've been saving them for a rainy day. And I guess maybe the clouds are gathering. Arthur can use them maybe to pay the doctor to look at my eyes. But if you get in any kind of scrape where you need to use one, you use it." He took three silver dollars out of his jeans pocket and laid them on the table. "You may need these. I'd like to give you more in case of need, but I'm down to hard pan."

It seemed to Laurie to be a great deal of money. She took her battered wallet out of her pocket. It had been her father's and it had his initials on it in gold. She put the silver dollars in it and she folded up the deed and put that in it too.

"I've got that silver chain of Mama's," she said. "I'll put the pouch with the gold nuggets on the chain and wear it around my neck. That way, I won't lose it."

"All right. You'd better start first thing in the morning. No sense wasting time once our minds are made up."

"How do I find Butte?" Except in her youngest years she had never been more than twenty-five miles from the cabin.

"You've got your compass, and I've got a map here. It's an old one, but I guess Butte hasn't moved any. I haven't been in that part of the country for a good many years, but I hear they got highways now. You'll have to get some shoes for Hook." He thought a minute. "Alec Begg's is the place to go."

She knew about Alec Begg. He was a blacksmith now, but he and Grandfather had had some high old times when they were younger. At one time they had driven a mule team on the Snake River Road. They had gone through a lot of adventures together.

"You trace it out on the map while I tell you." He waited till she got a pencil. "You ride east toward the north end of the lake. You'll come to a place called Jasper. It's not hardly what you'd call a town. Anyway Alec's got his place in Jasper, just south of town. You'll see it once you hit the dirt road."

"Doesn't it cost a lot of money to shoe a horse?" Laurie said.

"It ain't cheap," he said. "But I'll give you an I.O.U. for Alec. He'll take it. He and I have got each other out of plenty of tight spots before now."

Laurie found the place called Jasper on the map and marked it carefully. She looked at Butte. It looked like a long, long way. She was used to reading maps. She saved all the maps from the *Geographic* and tacked them up on her walls. She could find her way around the Holy Land if she had to, and she knew the names of all the countries in Africa. She guessed she could find Butte. She folded the map and put it in her pocket. She was getting more and more excited about making the trip.

"You'll need some things," her grandfather said. He sounded brisk for the first time in days, as if it felt good to be making decisions. "A blanket roll, a poncho. Your .22 and your hunting knife. A change of clothes. Plenty of matches. As much food as you can lug comfortably. We got a lot of jerky left; that'll come in handy. And some powdered milk and powdered eggs, salt, cornmeal, lard. A frying pan."

Laurie made a list on a piece of scrap paper. She was not worried about food. Her grandfather had long ago taught her how to live off the land. She knew what weeds and berries and wild flowers were edible, and she was a good shot.

"I'll make out fine," she said.

"Still and all, you might run into places where you couldn't get a rabbit or a squirrel, places close to towns. Stay as far away from those darned towns as you can."

"I will," she said. But she was curious to see a town, other than the tiny settlement ten miles away where she had been once or twice. She was excited about the idea of seeing Butte. Butte was a big city. "How will I find Uncle Arthur when I get there?"

"I got his address written down here." He gave her the piece of paper, and she added it to her wallet. "You'll have to ask somebody where it is. Don't ask a policeman. Pick out one of those gas stations and ask there. If you get lost, call him up and tell him to come get you."

Laurie wondered how you used a phone. But she

guessed she could figure it out if she had to.

"Will you be all right while I'm gone?"

" 'Course I will. I got all I need right here, and there's plenty of food."

"Be careful about the well," she said.

"Been going to that well for forty years," he said. "I guess I can manage a few more times." He tipped his chair back, beat twice on the table with his hand, and then began to sing in a strong baritone:

> It takes a worried man
> To sing a worried song.
> Oh, it takes a worried man
> To sing a worried song . . .

Laurie joined in with him.

> It takes a worried man
> To sing a worried song,
> I'm worried now
> But I won't be worried long.

They sang the next two verses together, and then he let his chair down with a thump and smiled broadly.

"You and me have gone through a lot together. They're not going to lick us now."

She came around the table and gave him a hug. She had never loved him more than she did at that moment. He was a tower of strength, and she was proud of him.

"Everything's going to turn out fine," she said. "I feel it in my bones."

"By jingo, I think you're right," he said heartily.

Later in the evening, while it was still light, she took

his mineral lamp and went out to the mine. She wanted to take another look at it now that she knew it was half hers.

The cold dampness struck her as soon as she stepped inside the portal. She flashed on the lamp and moved it around. Instantly the different minerals in the rock formations lit up in brilliant colors. It was fun to look at it all in the light of ownership.

On her way back to the cabin she stopped to say good night to Hook. "You're going on a long trip," she told him. "Get a good night's rest." She rubbed his velvety nose and stroked his sides. He was a beautiful bay, and she loved to curry him and keep him in top condition. "It's going to be very exciting," she said.

He nuzzled in her pocket until he found the usual lump of sugar.

"You'll have to learn to get along without sugar on this trip," she said. "We'll be traveling light. But when we get to Butte, I'll buy you a whole box." She kissed his nose and left him. Tomorrow at this time where would she be and what would she be doing?

chapter 3

"Take a loaf of that bread with you, too," her grand-father said. It was five o'clock on a cloudy morning, and she had her bedroll tied on behind her saddle and her rope coiled through the leather thong on the side of the saddle and her pack ready. Her rifle was in the case strapped to the other side of the saddle.

"I made the bread for you," she said.

"Three loaves! I can't eat all that before it goes stale. You take one."

She wrapped a loaf of the bread and shoved it into the pack, which was almost too full to hold it.

"By jingo," her grandfather said, "I believe you're ready for business." He was being very cheerful, but

Laurie was not fooled. She looked at him standing on the cabin step and felt a choking in her throat. She hugged him. "Take care of yourself."

His voice was a little gruff. "Don't worry about me. You just look after yourself. Remember everything I told you. Don't tell anybody anything—that's the safest way. Then they can't trip you up. Take your time and take it easy."

"I will," she said.

"I'm counting on you," he said.

"Everything will go just great," she said. "Don't you worry." She swung herself into the saddle. She had to get out of there fast or she would cry. She felt as if she were going away forever. "So long," she said.

He stood on the step waving. She stopped and looked back when she got to the edge of the forest. He looked small and far away, like someone seen through the wrong end of a spyglass. She had the feeling that she was leaving her old self behind—that whatever happened, she would be changed. She held Hook still a moment longer. "Good-bye," she said softly, and she was not sure whether she was saying good-bye to her grandfather or to herself.

"All right, Hook," she said. "All right, boy. Let's go!" She touched him lightly with the heels of her boots, and he broke into a fast trot.

When they reached the open meadow, the ghost town was no longer in sight. She let Hook run. They came into forest again on the other side, and he slowed down. She felt better there. It was going to be a wonderful adventure, and she was going to bring help to her grandfather. At great risk to life and limb, she thought. And then she corrected herself. Probably at not much risk at all. She had to watch herself because she had a tendency to dramatize everything. She often saw herself as Joan of Arc or Cleopatra or Ramona.

As she rode through the forest, the sun came out and the gray clouds thinned into white ones and then disappeared altogether except for a few shreds. The day grew warmer. The floor of the forest was covered with wild flowers, and the tall chokecherry bushes already had berries on them. Ordinarily in a month or so her grandfather would make chokecherry wine. Maybe he would tell her how to do it when she got back.

A fox ran across her path, and she held Hook for a moment to watch him. It was a red fox with a beautiful coat and bright inquisitive eyes. With a wave of his brush he was gone.

She was glad the sun was out because it made it easier to keep directions straight. For a while she would be on familiar territory, skirting the little settlement where her grandfather bought his groceries and got his mail. From there on it would be new ground.

When she came near the little town, she passed a man fishing in a creek. He looked up and waved. She waved back and kept on going. It made her a little nervous to be near the town. She hurried Hook to a faster trot.

Soon the town was behind them, and she relaxed. The way wound around the base of the mountains, and it was fairly open country. A stream, noisy with white water, rushed along beside her.

When the sun was high in the sky, she stopped for a few minutes and ate a sandwich that she had fixed before she left. She had a drink from her canteen and refilled it from the stream. Hook drank noisily from the creek, tossing his head and making a drama of it. She laughed at him, and he turned his head to look at her, his big dark eyes bright with intelligence. She thought he must be the finest horse that anybody had ever had.

As she rode on she came into forest again and had to slow down. There had been a forest fire there once. New trees had grown up, but every few feet a dead gray ghost of a tree reared up into the sky, too stubborn to fall. It gave the place an eerie look. She began to think about death. She had observed it so often, a deer falling dead at the crack of a rifle, a calf killed by a marauding mountain lion, a horse that had died when she was little. Each time she wondered and wondered about it. Lately it came into her mind sometimes that her grandfather would die some day. He was getting old, and old people died. Well, it didn't pay to think about that. She brushed her hair back from her eyes and spoke to Hook to speed him up a little.

In the afternoon she came to a battered sign that said, "Jasper, two miles". She followed the dirt road. As her grandfather had said, it was not much of a town. Two run-down gas stations and a bar and back from the road some sorry-looking houses. She looked curiously at the neon sign outside the bar. It said "JOE'S BAR", but the A didn't light up. She wondered why they wanted to go to all that trouble, to make those letters flash off and on. It would make your eyes ache if you looked at it very long. A man, coming out of the bar, walking unsteadily, stared at her.

"Hi, Sis," he said.

She didn't want to be rude so she nodded, but she urged Hook a little faster down the street. She wondered if the man was sick. He made her uneasy.

On the edge of town she came to Alec Begg's Blacksmith Shop. She was glad because she knew from the way Hook stepped that the hard-packed dirt road was hurting his unshod hooves. She turned into the blacksmith shop and slid down out of the saddle. The shop was a long, low sprawling place, with junk piled up against its sides. A sign said that Alec Begg also did welding. Inside the building she could see the orange glow of the forge. A small wiry man in a black leather apron was fitting a shoe to a horse. A boy, about eighteen or so, was holding the horse's head. Neither of them paid any attention to Laurie.

She stood just outside the shop wondering what to say. She coughed but the only response was a quick glance from the boy. He had shaggy yellow hair, and he looked mean. She couldn't see Alec Begg's face.

Finally Alec finished with the hoof and straightened up. "There you go," he said. The boy led the horse outside and tied him up.

"Mr. Begg?" Laurie said. What if it wasn't Mr. Begg at all? She had pictured him as a big powerful man, like the blacksmith in Longfellow's poem.

He turned toward her. He had a small leathery face, but his bright blue eyes were friendly.

"What can I do for you?"

She felt better. "I'm Peter Bent's granddaughter," she said. She fished out of her pocket the I.O.U. and the note that her grandfather had written. "He wondered if you would shoe my horse."

He held out a blackened hand for the note and looked at her closely. He read the note. Then he grinned. "So you're old Bent's grandchild, are you. How is the old boy?"

"Fine," she said. She knew Alec Begg was to be trusted, but it threw her off a little because he didn't look the way she had thought he would. In her grandfather's stories he had always come through sounding as if he were ten feet tall. Such a little wizened man just didn't seem like the Alec Begg she knew.

"Let's take a look at your horse," he said. He reached for the reins and Hook danced backward. "Whoo, boy," Alec said.

The boy with the raggedy blond hair reached out a long bony hand and shoved Hook on the rump. Hook snorted.

"Let him be," Alec said. "I got him." Soothingly he talked to the horse and then after a minute he stroked his nose. Hook rolled his eyes sideways to look at Laurie.

She put her hand on his neck. "It's all right," she said. Reluctantly Hook let himself be led into the dimness of the blacksmith shop.

Alec bent to look at Hook's hoof. His big hands were gentle. "Looks like a double-aught will do," he said. He nodded to the boy, who got some shoes down from the collection that hung on nails on the wall. Alec held it to Hook's hoof. Then he turned away toward the hot fire. Laurie wanted to watch how it was done, but she had to pay attention to Hook. The horse was nervous, and she was afraid he would bolt. He had never been shod before because she had not ridden him on roads. She didn't think it would hurt him, but she was a little worried.

Sparks in the furnace shot upward suddenly, and Hook reared. The shaggy-headed boy grabbed him and hit him sharply alongside his face. Hook snorted with pain and fear and jerked away from both of them and thundered out of the shop.

With all her might Laurie kicked the boy in the shin. He yelled and jumped backward. "Don't you dare touch my horse!" she said. Sick with anger, she ran out of the shop. Hook was heading for the road. Laurie whistled shrilly, and he stopped and turned his head toward her. She held out her hand and walked slowly toward him. He waited for her.

"Bring him back, Sis," Alec Begg said. He was standing in the entrance watching her.

For a moment she thought of just riding away. Nobody was going to manhandle her horse.

"Come on," he said. "I sent Johnny on out of here."

She picked up the reins and led Hook back to the shop. He had to have shoes. Hook pulled back on the reins, but she coaxed him inside.

"That's a mean, wicked boy," she said.

"He's a mite ornery," Alec said.

"Why do you let him work here?" She held Hook steady while Alec worked on the shoes.

"Well, sometimes boys are like horses—they start out wild and mean. You got to gentle 'em."

Laurie didn't say anything, but it was her private opinion that nobody would ever gentle that boy. If that was the way boys were, she didn't care to run into any more of them.

Finally Alec was through. He stood up and stroked Hook's nose. "Your grandfather always was a good hand at picking out a horse."

"I picked this one," she said.

He chuckled. "Just like the old man." He wiped his hands on his black leather apron. "Where you headin'?"

She hesitated. She didn't know whether her grandfather meant for her to tell Alec or not.

"Never mind," he said. "It was a nosey question."

Relieved, she said, "I really do thank you for shoeing the horse."

"Glad to do it," Alec said. "Old Bent's done me plenty of good turns. Is he gettin' along all right?"

"Yes," she said, "except he has a little trouble with his eyes. But he's going to get that fixed."

"Good. One of these days I'm goin' to ride out and see him. Always thought a lot of Bent." He helped her mount Hook. "Take care." He stood in the wide doorway of the shop watching her as she rode off down the street. She waved just before she turned the corner.

Hook was having a little trouble getting used to his shoes. He moved at an uneven gait at first. She stopped under a cottonwood tree to look at the map and get her bearings. She wanted to get away from the road. Cars went by every now and then, and Hook shied each time. She turned him off to the west, and they crossed a wooden bridge. Hook's shoes sounded like thunder on the boards. Then she turned south to follow the stream that chattered along. The ground was soft, and Hook regained his self-confidence. Now she could relax and let her mind wander.

chapter 4

It was still light when she decided to stop for the night. It would stay light until ten o'clock or so. Finding a good place to camp, she unsaddled Hook and led him down to the creek to drink and then tied him to a tree where there was plenty of grass for him to eat.

When she had found a sandy place to build her fire, she took out some of the cornmeal to make corn dodgers and she got out some of the jerky. For a liquid, she mixed some powdered milk with water in her collapsible cup. She was hungry, and it all tasted good.

When she was through she doused the fire and made up her bed near Hook. Using the saddle for a pillow, she wrapped herself in her blanket and lay back, looking up through the trees at the stars. The sky had some clouds in it now, and it looked soft and comfortable. Close by some frogs were harrumphing and several times an owl hooted. She wondered what the next day would be like.

She was almost asleep when she heard Hook whinny. She sat up. At first she could not see or hear anything unusual. Then in the dark branches about a dozen yards away she saw a tawny head with yellow gleaming eyes. It was a mountain lion. She reached for her gun and sat still, watching him. After a few minutes he turned and leaped away from her and disappeared. Hook stayed nervous for another fifteen or twenty minutes. Laurie sat watching. She didn't think the lion would attack her unprovoked, but it was a little uncomfortable to know he was around. Finally sleep overcame caution. She lay down on the ground and closed her eyes.

When she awoke, the sun was streaming through the trees and the birds were twittering their early morning racket.

She sat up and stretched. "Good morning, Hook," she said. He nickered. She went down to the creek and splashed cold water on her face. Further down the creek were the paw marks of the mountain lion. "He was just curious," she said. She built the fire up again and cooked some of the powdered eggs. Then she tore off a piece of bread and toasted it until it was golden brown. It would have been better with some butter.

During the morning as she rode along she came close to a highway where she could hear the cars whizzing past, and once she reined in on a ridge above the highway and watched them. She had not dreamed they would go so fast. Her grandfather had had an old pickup for a while but it had finally quit running and it stood now beside one of the cabins rusting. It had never gone more than thirty miles an hour. She tried to guess how fast these cars were going. Sixty? Seventy? More? She wondered what it felt like. She didn't think that she would like it, but she would like to try it. She had read about freeways and seen pictures of them. Now it was easier to imagine what they would be like.

"I like you better, Hook," she said.

The trail led away from the road again, back into the hills. In the afternoon it began to rain so she stopped and unrolled the poncho, draping it around herself and out behind her so that it would keep the blanket dry. Her head was exposed to the rain but she didn't mind. It felt cool and rather pleasant.

When she came to a place where the trees provided a shelter from the rain, she stopped. She slid out of the saddle and found a good spot for a fire. There were birch trees around and not far away a deadfall. She'd be able to start a fire in spite of the rain. She thought about making a lean-to but decided instead that she'd just roll up in her poncho under the most protecting trees. Her grandfather had taught her how to remove loose bark from a birch without damaging the tree. She got a broad sheet and put it in the most sheltered spot she could find and added handfuls of twigs, which she knew would burn even if they were wet. Then she pulled out some dry soft wood from inside the deadfall and added that, in a tipi shape. She covered the whole thing with more pieces of birch bark. The wind blew out her first two matches, but finally by lying on her stomach and shielding the match with her body she got the fire going. The black smoke curled up, and she felt rather pleased with herself. She had helped her grandfather build such fires many times, but this was the first one she had done all alone.

The fire felt good. She ate some jerky again and made some more corn dodgers and heated some milk. It felt cozy there in the shelter of the trees. Hook stood near her, lazily eating away at some bushes. Laurie toasted a piece of bread and ate it. She covered up the rest of the loaf and set it on top of the pack until she decided whether she wanted another piece.

In the clearing just beyond the place where she sat, she could see occasional flashes of lightning and then she would listen to the roll of thunder. She had always liked thunderstorms. The fire was burning with a nice steady glow, sizzling sometimes when a shower of raindrops fell from the trees. It was not raining as hard as it had been.

She was beginning to get sleepy when suddenly there was a close, vivid flash of lightning, and in its light she saw a man sitting on a mule in the clearing. She was so startled, she jumped to her feet. He was a strange-looking man, so tall that his feet seemed almost to touch the ground. He was covered up with a black poncho and on his head he wore a big black wide-brimmed hat. When the lightning was gone, she could see him only as a dark silhouette. He was looking in her direction.

Instinctively she moved over to Hook and put her hand on her gun. The man pulled his mule around and rode toward her. Laurie's hand closed tighter on the stock of the gun.

When he was quite close, he said, "Good evening, sister," in a deep loud voice.

"Good evening," Laurie said.

He swung down off his mule. "I saw the light of your fire. And I said to myself, 'God showeth the way to a poor wayfaring stranger'." He held out his hands to the flames.

Laurie relaxed a little. He reached over to her pack and picked up the loaf of bread, unwrapped it, broke off a piece and chewed on it. "You won't mind sharing with a man who's a little down on his luck," he said.

"I don't have much to share," Laurie said. She didn't like his grabbing her bread like that.

"That's all right. You know the story of the loaves and the fishes. The good Lord made do. We'll make do."

"But I don't know how to perform miracles," Laurie said. "Do you?"

The man stopped chewing for a moment to look at her. He had a very long face with deep lines in it. His eyes seemed to be deep in his head, and they had a strange brightness. "I have performed miracles in my time," he said, nodding. "Minor miracles, to be sure, but miracles. You must have faith."

"Are you a preacher?" Laurie asked.

"Yes," he said, "you might say that. I go the length and the breadth of the land preaching the word of the Lord." He opened her pack and looked inside. He pulled out a piece of jerky and began to eat it. He had big hands with long bony fingers.

Laurie was trying not to be angry. Maybe with a preacher you were supposed to share what you had. It wasn't so much that she minded sharing, though, as the fact that he just took without asking. "What church do you belong to?" she said.

He was sitting hunkered down on his heels. He looked

up at her with that same intense look. "I don't belong to no church. I bring the word direct from the Lord. He told me to spread the news, and I'm spreading the news."

"What news?" she said.

"Why, the news of His greatness. The news of man's wickedness. The news of the world's destruction. Do you read the Bible?"

"Yes, I do," she said.

"It's all there in Revelations. Have you got anything else to eat?"

"No," Laurie said.

He went to his saddlebags and got a can of beans. From a sheath attached to his boot he pulled out a wicked-looking knife that had a hooked blade. Using it to punch holes in the top of the can, he set the can at the edge of the fire to heat.

"You had food of your own all the time," Laurie said.

He looked past her as if he was seeing things in the forest that no one else could see. "The four horsemen of the Apocalypse will come," he said, "to destroy this sinful world." His black hair was long and shaggy under the black hat, and he wore sideburns that came almost to the corners of his mouth.

"I hope not," Laurie said. "I think it's a nice world."

He focussed his burning gaze on her face. "Sister," he said, "you wallow in ignorance. When you have traveled the length and breadth of the land as I have done, when you have seen what I have seen . . ." He broke off. "Where are you headed for?"

Taken by surprise Laurie hesitated. Then she said, "Down south of here a ways."

"I am returning to Butte," he said. "I too travel south.

We will travel together."

Laurie was alarmed. "Oh no," she said, "I couldn't do that. I'm in an awful hurry."

"The whole world is in a hurry," he said. "Hurrying toward destruction."

"My horse goes quite fast," she said. "Faster, I guess, than your mule. I really have to hurry."

As if he had not heard her, he said, "We will travel together, and I will protect you from the sins of the world."

"Thank you very much," Laurie said, "but I really must go alone."

He was looking at her throat. "What do you carry in that little sack around your neck?" he said.

Laurie glanced down. The pouch containing the gold nuggets had slipped outside the front of her shirt. "Oh, it's just something I carry," she said. "It isn't anything."

He stood up. He looked ten feet tall. He came over to her. She tried to pull away but his bony hand grasped the pouch and pulled the drawstring. He stared at the nuggets for a moment. His face was transfigured. "Gold!" he said in a whisper. "Gold!"

Laurie pulled away from him and closed the pouch. "Don't touch them," she said. He started toward her again, and she pulled her hunting knife from the scabbard that hung from her belt. She pointed it toward him. "Don't come near me." His own knife lay by the fire where he had put it down.

He stopped. Then he threw back his head and laughed, a deep triumphant laugh. "The Lord does provide," he said. "God moves in many mysterious ways his wonders to perform."

"These are not mine," she said. "You must not touch them."

"Of course they aren't yours," he said. "They belong to God. All the birds of the air and the beasts of the fields and the minerals of the earth, they are all, all God's." He went back and sat by the fire and began eating his beans with his fingers. "We will study on the proper use for that gold," he said.

There was no use arguing with him. He was, she was sure, quite crazy. She would just have to figure out how to escape. She stayed near Hook in case she saw a chance.

When he had finished eating, the man threw the empty can over his shoulder into the bushes. The fire had begun to die down, but Laurie made no move to build it up. The man took out a cigarette and began to smoke. The smoke had a sickish sweet smell, not at all like the smoke from her grandfather's cigarettes or pipe.

He looked up and saw her watching him. He pointed to the cigarette. "The Lord gave us these," he said, "so that we might get closer to his glory." He leaned his head back and began to sing in a high thin voice:

> This is my story,
> This is my song.
> Praise for my Savior
> All the day long.

He sang it over and over again. Behind him lightning flickered along the mountain tops and thunder rumbled.

Laurie waited. After a while the words of his song became garbled. The pupils of his strange eyes seemed to dilate. She wished she could get at her gun without causing him to notice. She didn't know exactly what she would do with it if she had it. She knew she could never shoot anybody, but a shot might scare him off. He terrified her because he was so irrational. With a rational person, even a wicked one, it seemed to her you could reason; but how could you reason with someone like this?

"I am the Lord's faithful servant," the man said suddenly. His head had fallen forward on his knees but now he jerked up straight and glared at her. "I fulfill the word of the Lord. I am he of the second coming." Then he began to sing again, "This is my story, this is my song . . ."

Cold chills ran down Laurie's back. "God," she said in her mind, "God, take this faithful servant off my hands. I am afraid of him."

She waited. The rain stopped and after a while the moon showed dimly through some ragged clouds. She waited.

Just when she thought the man was asleep, he reared up again and cried in a loud voice, "I see the golden stairway! I see the throne!" Then his head fell forward on his chest again.

She waited. After about an hour when he had not moved, she got up very carefully. The fire had died down to embers. She knew she ought to put it out but she didn't dare risk waking him. In all this wetness there was, she hoped, no danger of fire spreading. Water dripped from the trees.

She got to her knees. If she could just quietly get on Hook and ride away while the man still slept. . . . She got to her feet. He had not moved. She moved toward

Hook. Just as she reached him, the mule gave a raucous "hee-haw" and the man jumped to his feet.

Laurie leaped into the saddle. The man ran at her. He grabbed her stirrup. She got her foot loose and kicked at him, but he got her ankle in his hard fist. She felt his fingers dig into her flesh.

He was screaming. "Jezebel! Jezebel!"

Hook was shaking his head and pawing the ground. Still the man hung on. Laurie pulled her rifle out of the holster.

"Let go of me," she said.

He did not let go. He pulled on her, trying to pull her out of the saddle. She aimed the rifle at the ground near his feet and fired. He leaped back with such a great scream that she thought for a moment she had hit him. But she saw the torn-up place in the dirt where the bullet had struck. She wheeled Hook around and dug her heels into his sides.

He set off at a run. She clung to his neck, bending her head low to avoid being struck by branches. She let him run for a long time.

She had the feeling that the man was right behind her, although she was sure that no mule could travel as fast as Hook could. When she came to a little lake she slowed him down, breathing hard. It was dark in the forest, but the moonlight filtered through the trees. It was better to keep going. She rode around the shore of the lake and then struck off again into the woods. There was a tent in the distance, but she carefully skirted it. She wondered how long she would have to ride before it would be safe to stop.

chapter 5

She slept at last in a mossy hollow. When she awoke the next morning, the sun was already well up. She sat up with a jerk, afraid of seeing that spectral figure, of hearing that song. After a hasty breakfast, she rode without incident through most of the day, keeping an eye out for mule tracks.

Once she had to cross a dirt road. There were farmhouses strung out along the road, and at one of them a man was plowing, but he did not look up.

Late in the afternoon, dead tired, she came to another lake. It was a pretty lake, the water a deep green. Birches hung over it. She made a camp on a knoll overlooking the lake and then went down to the water to wash and have a swim. She took her change of clothes and a bar of soap. At the lake she shed the jeans and shirt that were dirty and still damp from the previous day. But first she let Hook drink and wallow around in the water to get cool and then she tied him to a birch. Finally she plunged into the lake and swam. It felt wonderfully cold and fresh. Her fatigue melted away. She came out and got the soap and lathered herself thoroughly. When she was clean, she washed her clothes.

After she had put on her dry clean clothes, she found that she was ravenously hungry and could hardly wait to fix supper. "Do you want to stay here?" she asked Hook. "There's good long grass." He raised his head and shook his mane. Then suddenly he turned his head and tensed. He was looking up the slope. He whinnied and tried to pull loose. Laurie felt her blood run cold.

"What's the matter?" she said. He pulled nervously. She was afraid to go and look but she had to do it. She went up the slope, trying to keep out of sight. As she came upon her camp site, she saw a big brown bear pawing at her knapsack. She was so relieved that it was a bear and not the man that she leaned weakly against the nearest tree. Her food was strewn all over the ground. The bear saw her and glared at her with his small baleful eyes.

She did not trust bears. Once her grandfather had been attacked by a bear and had had to shoot it. Her gun lay on the ground near where the bear was standing. Anyway she would never trust herself to shoot a bear with a .22. It would only wound him and infuriate him. At least this was not a grizzly. She waited to see what he would do. He rose up on his hind legs and started moving slowly toward her.

"Take it easy, bear," she said in a soothing voice. "Go on about your business. Go on home." She waited and he stopped, waving his head from side to side. "At least I'd rather face you than the lone wayfaring stranger," she said. She waited and waited. She could hear Hook whinnying excitedly. Horses hated bears.

Finally the bear dropped down to all four feet, swung his awkward body around and lumbered off into the trees. She stood still a minute longer to make sure he was gone and then she went to look at the havoc he had wrought.

The powdered eggs and milk were spilled all over the ground. He had trampled the last of the jerky under his big paws. There was nothing left except a can of Spam and a handful of cornmeal strewn around the bottom of her pack. Opening the Spam she ate it cold. Then she went down to say good night to Hook.

"It was just an old bear," she said. "The food's gone and I'm still hungry, but I'm too tired to think about it tonight. Tomorrow we'll figure out what to do." She put her cheek against his nose. "Just pray that that man doesn't show up again." She patted him and went back to her camp.

She slept uneasily that night, listening even in her sleep. Several times she awoke with a start thinking she heard something but it was only a small animal scurrying through the bushes.

When she awoke in the morning, she sat bolt upright. A man was standing there looking at her. It was not the man she was afraid it would be, but a big man in a plaid shirt and jeans and waders, with a fishing pole in his hand and a creel slung over his shoulder. He had a round red face.

"Hello there." He smiled.

He had crooked teeth and he needed a shave. "Camping out?" he said. It seemed like a foolish question, and she did not answer it. He laughed. "Kind of bashful, are you?" He looked at the blanket she was wrapped in. "If you're going to camp out, you ought to do it right. Get yourself a sleeping bag. Then you can sleep real cozy. I got one down to my store I can let you have real cheap. Had a fire in my place a while back and some things got kind of smoky. This sleeping bag, it smells of smoke but it ain't damaged any. Let you have it for three dollars."

She wondered if in some mysterious way he knew that she had three silver dollars. She shook her head. "I don't need one."

"Saw your horse down by the lake," he said. "That's a nice-looking horse."

She nodded, wishing desperately that he would go away. She thought about making a run for Hook, but the man could easily catch her. What did he want?

"I got a girl about your age," he said, "but she don't like camping worth a darn. All that equipment I got and she don't want no part of it." He shook his head. "People are different." He studied her. "You ain't running away from home, are you?"

"No," she said.

"Your folks know where you are?"

"Yes."

"That's good. Because that would be a foolish thing to run away from home." He looked at the food that the bear had strewn on the ground. "Looks like some critter got to your grub."

"A bear," she said. He saw too much. It made her nervous. He seemed friendly enough but that might be

43

just a pose. For all she knew, he might be the sheriff.

He opened his creel and took out two rainbow trout. "Maybe you can use these."

"No, thank you," she said. "I'm all right. Really, I have plenty to eat."

He laid them on some pine needles. "I'll just leave them here anyway in case you change your mind. I know kids your age can get powerful hungry." He put the creel strap back over his shoulder. "And if you want to come on into town after a while and buy that sleeping bag, my place is right on the main street. Monty's Sporting Goods. If I ain't there, tell the boy I said you could have that bag for three dollars. Take care of yourself now and enjoy them fish." He strode off toward the east and soon he had disappeared among the trees.

Quickly she got her things together. She looked at the fish. She was awfully hungry. There was no point in leaving them there to spoil. She wrapped them in leaves and put them in her pack. When she had saddled Hook, she rode off at a fast trot.

They pushed on for an hour before she felt it was safe to stop. Then she built a fire and cooked the fish. They tasted very good. As soon as she had eaten, she put out the fire. In case the wayfaring stranger was anywhere around, she didn't want him to see the smoke and find her. She had the feeling that he was on her trail, and it made her very uneasy. She knew he wanted her gold.

It was a beautiful day, and she rode on trying to shake off her nervousness by singing one of her grandfather's favorite songs:

> I got a home in Beulah land
> That outshines the sun.

44

I got a home in Beulah land
That outshines the sun.
I got a home in Beulah land
That outshines the sun,
Away beyond the blue.

She sang all the verses, and it made her feel better. The sun was bright and the air seemed to sparkle. She felt sorry for people who didn't live in Montana. It would be nice to see a little of the world but afterwards she would want to go back to Hawkins Dry Diggings and live there forever.

In the afternoon she stopped to look for food. She found some wild spinach near a creek, and she gathered an armful and cooked it. Pigweed, some called it, but she thought wild spinach was a nicer name. It was not very filling, but it was better than nothing.

She rode on again, letting Hook take his own pace. He jogged along at a fast walk. There were foothills alongside the trail now, some of them covered with conifers, some of them with rocks.

Once she rode a little way up a hill to see the lay of the land. Off to the east there was a lake that seemed to go on forever. She would have liked to get a good look at it but there was a highway in the way, so she decided against it.

The trail was wide and grassy and pleasant to ride on. She relaxed in the saddle, getting a little sleepy. Then suddenly she stiffened. A voice, somewhere behind her, was singing:

This is my story,
This is my song. . . .

She risked a backward look. The stranger on the mule had just come into sight. When he saw her, he pulled up the mule short for a second, and then he dug his heels into its sides and yelled.

"Run!" Laurie said to Hook. Hook bolted forward into a run.

"Wait! Stop!" She could hear the man yelling. And she could hear the pounding of the mule's hooves.

She leaned forward in the saddle and rode like the wind. But Hook was tired; she couldn't run him that fast too long. She saw a small mountain ahead of her, covered with big rocks. The approach to it was loose shale; it wouldn't show hoofprints. Sharply she turned Hook into the shale and forced him up the side of the mountain. Halfway up, she stopped at a rock that was big enough to conceal both Hook and her, and slipped out of the saddle, pulling Hook behind the rock. She was breathing hard. She took her gun out of the holster and held it ready, just in case.

In a few minutes she heard the thundering of the mule. She put her hand over Hook's muzzle so he wouldn't whinny. The man and the mule came into sight. Laurie made herself small. The man was wearing a black coat that fluttered behind him, and the heavy awkward gait of the mule threw him around in the saddle. His hair streamed out in back beneath the shapeless hat. He rode past Laurie's hiding place, and then abruptly he stopped. She held her breath.

He stood up in his stirrups and looked all around. "Hey!" he yelled. "Hey!" He shaded his eyes to see in every direction. Once he looked toward her hiding place, but he didn't see her. "I'll find you," he yelled. "I'll find you." He slapped the mule and rode on.

When she dared to, Laurie scrambled a little farther up the rocky hill to see if she could see him. There he was, looking small and black, thundering down the trail. He came to a junction where the trail went straight ahead and a gravel road veered off to the east. She saw him rein in the mule and look in all directions. Then he went on down the trail.

She went back and got Hook. "We'll have to go down the road then," she said. "It probably goes to a town, but it's safer than running into him." She was trembling so much it was hard to make her knees work properly as she went down the hill. It wasn't just that this man was after her gold; there was something evil about him—the way he talked, the strange way he quoted the Bible and sang hymns, the way he flapped along on his mule like a huge black bird. He filled her with terror.

For a moment, when he rode past her and then stopped, she could have shot him. She had felt her fingers tighten on the gun. Maybe that was part of the evil, that he tempted people to do terrible things. She shivered.

When she came to the gravel road, she took it, looking back often over her shoulder. He might change his mind and come back this way. She was glad when she came to the highway that ran along the lake. There were cottages now and then and sometimes a car went by. She kept Hook as far to the right of the road as she could, up on the grass.

The lake was very big and there were a lot of boats on it. Boats that went fast with a lot of noise. She had never thought about boats having motors, like cars. It seemed strange that people wanted to go so fast on such a pretty lake. There were sailboats, too, silent and beautiful. The only boat she had ever seen was a raft that her grandfather had built, that they had taken down river a few times. It had been wonderful fun.

When no cars were in sight, she crossed the road and went down a grassy slope to the lake, to take a closer look. Those noisy boats kept going in big circles. What fun was that? She liked the sailboats that looked like big birds. Then she saw a girl being towed behind a fast boat —standing on something, Laurie decided, though at first she thought the girl was just skimming along on top of the water with her bare feet. She shaded her eyes so she could see. They looked like skiis. Water skiis! The girl went like the wind.

"Gosh," Laurie said to Hook, "I'd like to try that sometime."

A woman came walking down to the landing. She looked at Laurie curiously and said hello . Startled, Laurie nodded and turned Hook's head back toward the road. Everywhere you went, somebody showed up. What an unnatural way to live. The more she saw of the outside world, the more she liked her own. Except for a few things like that skiing on water, she much preferred her own place. And now that she was actually on her way to Butte, she felt reassured about her grandfather. Uncle Arthur would get him all fixed up and then things would be the way they had always been again.

The houses began to be closer together. She wondered how people could stand to live so close. A man could stand in his own back yard and spit into his neighbor's yard without half trying.

She got into the commercial part of town where there

were gas stations and stores, a restaurant, a small hotel, some bars. She slowed Hook down and tried to look as if she belonged here. There were not many people on the street, and no one paid any attention to her, so she decided it was going to be all right. When she got to the southern end of town, she felt even more confident because the buildings were more strung out.

She saw a little grocery store, and it struck her that she could spend one of her silver dollars for food. In one way it seemed like a foolish extravagance, but it would save her time. Sometimes it took a while to hunt down a rabbit or a squirrel. She decided to do it.

After she had hitched Hook to a little iron bridge that spanned a narrow rushing creek, she went into the store. As soon as she got inside, she wished she hadn't gone. A man looked up from behind the counter, where he was reading a newspaper, and said "hello". She said, "hello" and walked to the far side of the store. He made her nervous. She knew he was watching her, and now that she was there, she had no idea of what to buy. She hadn't known that stores had so much stuff in them.

"Can I help you find something?" the man said.

"No, thanks," she said. Maybe he thought she was going to steal something. What if he called the police? Maybe she looked like a suspicious character. She got very hot and she wanted to bolt out of the store, but that would look even worse. She had to buy something—anything. She picked up a can marked Vienna Sausage, not knowing what they were, a box of crackers, and a bunch of bananas. Then she was frightened because she had not checked the prices. What if they came to more than three dollars?

The man punched keys on a little machine and looked at the slip of paper. "Will that be all?" he said.

"Yes." She fished in her pocket to make sure her money was still there.

"That will be eighty-five cents," he said.

She slid one of the dollars toward him. He looked at it and she thought he was not going to accept it. "These things are getting scarce," he said.

She didn't know what to say. Perhaps he meant they weren't any good.

"I know a feller collects them," he said. "He figures on cleaning up one of these days."

She didn't know what he meant and she wished he would hurry. It seemed like hours before he finally rang

up the sale and dropped the silver dollar into the cash register. He gave her her change and put the groceries in a paper sack. "There you are," he said.

She picked up the sack and almost ran out of the store. She stuffed the things into her pack, unhitched Hook, and rode off down the street. She had the feeling that she had had a narrow escape, and yet the more she thought about it, the more she realized that nothing really had happened or even threatened to happen. I'm just getting skittish, she thought.

On the outskirts of the town she saw a tiny church set back from the road a little, shaded by box elder trees. It looked cool. On an impulse she turned in. It would be good to pull herself together for a minute and cool off. She hitched Hook and went and sat down on the wooden step. She hoped nobody would mind. There was a little house next to the church, but she didn't see anyone.

She leaned her back against the warm dark wood of the door and gradually began to relax. She was going to have to make up her mind not to worry so much about the stranger. She couldn't ride all the way to Butte in a state of terror. It was probably her own imagination that made him so scary. If she ran into him again, she would just tell him to leave her alone. But she shivered as she thought of running into him again and she knew it would not be that simple.

A door opened in the little house and a young priest came out. He was carrying two bottles of Coke. He came over to her, and she wondered if he was going to tell her that sitting on the church step was not allowed.

"Hi," he said.

She had never seen a priest in person, and she would never have expected one to say "hi".

"Hello," she said.

He sat down beside her. "I saw you sitting out here, and I thought you might like a Coke." He held it out to her.

Her grandfather once in a while brought home Coke and she loved it. "Thanks," she said.

"It's a hot day." He tipped up his bottle and drank.

The bottle felt frosty and good on Laurie's hands, and when she drank, she realized how thirsty she had been.

"Are you new in town?" He said it casually, not as if he were prying.

She glanced sideways at him. He had a high forehead and a Roman nose and he was quite handsome.

"I'm just riding through."

He nodded, and they sat for a few minutes in silence.

"Would you like to see the inside of the church?" he said. "It's quite old and interesting."

"Yes."

They went inside. It was cool and dim. There were rows of dark high-backed pews and up front, at what she supposed was the holy end, there was an altar and a cross. There was a high pulpit and another raised place that looked like the pulpit but was not as high.

"You're not a Catholic, are you?" he said.

"No."

He explained to her the stations of the cross and the faded paintings on the ceiling. "A French priest started this church for the Indians," he said. "We still have a lot of Indian parishioners."

She looked at the altar with great interest. It seemed so

quiet there. She wanted to ask him about holy communion, which she had read about but never really understood, but she was shy about asking him.

When they went outside again, she said, "Do you believe in the devil?" She hadn't planned to say that, and it surprised her to hear herself.

"Yes," he said.

They sat down on the steps again. "Do you believe that he just goes riding around the country, on a mule, for instance?" She looked at him quickly to see if he was going to laugh at her.

He looked at her curiously, but he didn't smile. "I've never encountered him in just that way," he said, "but I suppose he takes many forms."

"What would you do if you ran into him?"

"If I were a young girl, I guess I'd pray and run. Simultaneously." He watched her face for a moment. "Did you run into him?"

She didn't want to get too far into this. "Oh, once," she said casually.

After a minute he said, "That's a pretty horse."

"He's a jim-dandy." She got up. "I guess I'd better be going."

He walked with her to where Hook was standing and helped her into the saddle.

"I'm glad you stopped by," he said. "I enjoyed talking with you."

"Thanks, I enjoyed it, too."

He put his hand on Hook's neck. "And if you run into the devil again, I'd suggest you make tracks for the nearest policeman."

She nodded. "Thanks for the Coke."

He lifted his hand, and she rode away. She looked back once but he was gone. As she rode, she thought about what he had said about a policeman. You didn't run into policemen out in the woods. Besides, if the stranger was really the devil, no jail would hold him. She would just have to look out.

The priest had been nice. She wondered what it was like to be a priest. You'd have people on your hands all the time, and you'd have to put up with them. From what Grandfather said, you couldn't tell what people would be like.

A truck roared by and Hook shied so badly that he almost unseated her. So she went up a side street to get away from the road, then down another street that angled in. When it turned out to be dead end, and the land beyond it heavily fenced, she backed around and tried another dirt street. It was no better. She seemed to be caught in a regular maze of roads and lanes that wound around and crossed over each other. Why couldn't folks be more orderly? At Hawkins Dry Diggings the paths were laid out neatly just like geometry.

There were a lot of poor-looking houses along the streets, unpainted and untidy. Some of them had tipis in their back yards, and in one there were some Indian children playing, and a dog ran out to bark at her. That made her feel as if she were all right. She felt safe with Indians. But she was lost. She didn't know how to get out of such a warren of streets. Then a boy about eight years old rode out of a yard on a bony pinto. He had a round face and very black eyes. He looked at her without expression.

"I'm lost," she said. "Will you help me?"

chapter 6

The boy rode off without a word, and she thought he was not going to help her. Then he looked back and said, "Come on."

She followed him as he rode down one dusty street and then another until finally he stopped. "Where you want to go?" he said.

"I want to get out of town. I'm heading south."

"You want the highway?"

"No."

He pulled his horse over in front of Hook. Hook snorted with annoyance.

"Be quiet," Laurie said to him.

The boy led her down one street after another, crisscrossing and sometimes it seemed to her, backtracking. They crossed a rickety bridge, and when they had crossed the creek he turned his horse south, leading across a wide meadow sprinkled with blue-flowering weeds. When they came to the forest, he turned his horse into a faintly marked trail and pulled up.

"If you follow this trail, you can see the highway most of the time," he said.

"How far does the trail go?"

"I don't know. I've never gone to the end of it. You want me to come along with you for a ways?"

"If you want to," she said. They rode along side by side. "What's your name?" she said.

He looked at her with his shiny black eyes. "I am called Robert at school but my real Indian name is Kicking Horse."

"That's a good name," she said.

"What's yours?"

"Laurie." She ducked to miss an overhanging branch of a mountain ash. She wished she had a name like Kicking Horse.

"Do you like school?"

"No," he said contemptuously. "I like to hunt and fish. And dance. Last year at the Pow Wow I won second place in the boys' contest."

"That's very good," she said. "I would like to go to a Pow Wow sometime."

He nodded. "It's very nice."

"I wish I were an Indian," Laurie said.

He shook his head. "It is not so good to be an Indian now. In the old days it was good. My grandfather says it was very good."

"What tribe do you belong to?"

"Salish."

"I have some good friends who are Blackfeet," she said.

"Salish are better."

"Do you have brothers and sisters?"

"Eight brothers, two sisters."

"Jingo," she said, "that must be something." She tried to imagine growing up with all those children. She decided it was better just to have a grandfather and a horse.

"My mother says too many mouths to feed."

"Do you have a father?"

"No. He went to California when the last baby was born. He never came back."

"He'll probably come back some day and take you all to California with him."

"He'd be a fool to do that," Kicking Horse said.

They rode on in companionable silence for a while. Then when they came to another open field, Laurie said, "Do you want to see how fast my horse can trot?"

"Sure."

She urged Hook to a fast trot. When they reached the other side of the field, she pulled up and waited for Kicking Horse, whose horse came up at an awkward loose-gaited gallop.

"I never saw a horse trot like that," he said.

"He's part Hambletonian. They're trained to be trotters. What they're really trained for is to pull little two-wheeled carts. If you're going to ride a Hambletonian, you have to learn to sit him right. It took me a long time to learn. He used to bounce the daylights out of me." She was enjoying being able to talk freely to someone without having to worry.

"Someday I'm going to get me the best horse there is," Kicking Horse said.

"Your horse is nice," Laurie said politely.

"He's just a bag of old bones." The boy was scornful. "Someday I'm going to catch me a wild horse up in the hills and train him myself."

Kicking Horse was very small. Laurie tried to imagine him breaking a wild horse.

"Would you like a banana?" she said. "I've got some in my pack."

His face lit up. "Sure."

They slid off their horses, and she opened up her pack and took out the bunch of bananas. Breaking off the biggest one, she gave it to him. He ate as if he hadn't eaten in a long time. His banana was gone before she was half-finished. She gave him another one, and he ate that with the same speed and efficiency.

He sighed. "I better go back now. I got to go to work."

"What do you do?"

"I set up pins in a bowling alley." He said it with pride.

Laurie had no idea what a bowling alley was, but she did not like to ask. "Is it a good job?"

"Yes, but the man, he says he is going to get one of them automatic pin-setters. Then I won't have no job."

"Maybe you'll find a better one."

He shrugged as if he did not put much faith in that idea.

"Well, I got to go."

"Thanks for showing me the way," she said.

"Where are you going anyway?" He scrambled back

onto his horse.

"To Butte."

His eyes widened. "That's a long way."

"I know it. But I got to go there."

"If it wasn't for my mother, I'd go with you. I'd like to go to Butte. It's a big city." His face was thoughtful for a moment. Then he shook his head. "But my mother, she would give me a terrible licking." His glance fell on the remaining bananas.

Laurie picked them up. There were five left. "Here, you take them." She put them in his arms.

He grinned broadly. He had a missing front tooth, and his smile changed his expression and made him look mischievous.

"Laurie," he said, "I'll never forget you. I'll name a dance for you."

"That would be great," she said. "And I won't forget you either, Kicking Horse. I hope you get your wild pony."

He clapped his heels into the skinny sides of the pinto. The horse took off with his lopsided run. Laurie watched them across the field, hating to see him go. When he reached the far side, he turned, thrust one arm high in the air, and pulled his horse up on his hind legs. Laurie waved both arms. Then Kicking Horse was gone.

chapter 7

As she rode along she could hear the sounds of the highway. The world was certainly noisy. She began to think about what it must have been like in the days of the Indians. She wished it were still that way. She had read in her father's books about the Indians being cheated, and it made her mad. There was Kicking Horse, eight years old, working in a bowling alley when he should be getting ready to count *coup*. She'd have to ask her grandfather what a bowling alley was.

When she was ready to stop for the night, she looked until she found a place where no one would be likely to see her. Once settled, she ate all the crackers and the can of Vienna Sausages. The sausages were pretty good, but it seemed sinful to charge all that money for a few little dabs of meat. Sometimes she thought about how she could make a little money so her grandfather wouldn't have to worry. Now she decided that maybe she could smoke some of the fish and meat they caught and sell it to stores. If people would pay as much as they did for a little old can of Vienna Sausages, think what they might pay for good home-smoked salmon or bear meat.

She was still hungry and she wished she had kept just one banana. But she hadn't, so there was nothing to do but sleep. Before she lay down, she listened carefully. There were no sounds except the night sounds of the forest. So she went to sleep and dreamed that she had ten brothers and sisters and they played games all day long. They had to teach her how to play the games and she was afraid they wouldn't like her because she was slow in learning.

She woke up still in the grip of anxiety from the dream. The sky looked threatening. Big storm clouds piled up over the mountains, and it was much colder. She put on her jacket and thought about breakfast. There was nothing left except some loose cornmeal in the bottom of her pack. She shook it out into the frying pan, added some water, and shaped little cakes. There was still the can of lard. In a few minutes she had a small fire going, and the corn dodgers were frying. She let them get crisp and brown. The cornmeal had some dirt in it from the bottom of the pack and she had had to pick out some pine needles, but she was too hungry really to mind. She ate every crumb. The next time she stopped at a store, if she ever got up nerve enough to stop again, she'd have to get something sensible like cornmeal or flour.

The meal finished, she scrubbed the frying pan with sand. When she was packed and ready to go, she looked up at the sky. There was a storm coming all right. It looked like a thunderstorm. She was glad she had the poncho and if it got too bad, maybe she could find a cave or something where she could sit it out.

Within half an hour, it had begun to rain. Lightning flickered over the mountains and thunder rumbled. She put on the poncho and kept going. Hook tossed his head and looked back at her.

"You're not scared of a little rain, are you?" she said. But she knew he did not like thunderstorms. He nickered and she patted his neck.

"You're a good old boy."

The rain began coming down very hard. She crossed a dirt road that was already turning muddy. The lightning was much closer and the thunder smashed. Hook, very nervous, shied at each crash of thunder. The rain was coming down in such solid sheets it was hard for her to see. She looked around for a possible shelter but all she could see were a couple of farmhouses, and she didn't want to go there.

She rode on doggedly, the trail turning finally into some semblance of a road, with tire marks. Then it came out of the trees and became a dirt road. There was a tremendous crash of thunder, and the sky opened up, the rain pounding down and then turning to hail. The hailstones were small at first but they got bigger, bouncing off her saddle, off her head, off Hook. They were big enough to hurt. A particularly large one struck Hook in the head, and he reared. She tried to calm him. She had to get them inside somewhere before they really got hurt. It was very dark, but in a flash of lightning she saw a big barn down the road and headed for it.

Noticing a gray board-and-batten house a little distance from the barn, she hoped that whoever lived there was not watching. She pushed open the heavy barn door and led Hook inside and closed the door. It was dark, and for a moment she could not see anything, but it was a relief to be out of the pounding hail. "Bigger'n baseballs," her grandfather always said when it hailed.

She had never seen a real barn before, and she was amazed at how big it was. At home they just had a corral for the horses and some sheds to keep things in. This barn had four empty stalls and there was a small car parked in the middle of the barn, such a tiny car, she wondered if it was real. A person could live in a place as big as this. There were shelves with neatly arranged cans of paint and tools. It was very clean. She guessed it had been a long time since animals had used the barn. There was a hayloft but as far as she could see there was no hay in it.

She got her shirt out of the pack and used it to rub down Hook. Afterwards he let her lead him into one of the stalls. She sat down on the floor and wrapped her arms around herself. She was still shivering, wet, and cold. The hailstones still bounced off the roof. And every few minutes there was a blinding flash and a boom as the lightning struck somewhere nearby. Then the hail seemed to let up, but the rain kept coming down in a hard incessant drumming.

Suddenly she heard unearthly screams from somewhere in back of the barn. They sounded like a woman in terrible pain or fear. Laurie's throat tightened and she stood up, but she didn't know what to do. She waited and the screaming stopped. She would have to do something. Someone must be in terrible trouble. She took a step toward the door. The scream came again. She stood still trying to figure out just where it came from.

Then slowly the barn door began to open.

chapter 8

Laurie froze. She could feel the tingling in her wrists that came with terror. The door swung open, and in the dim light stood someone swathed in a long raincoat, carrying an umbrella. Laurie took a cautious step backward. Perhaps she could hide in one of the stalls.

But the beam of a flashlight flared in the dark of the barn. The light moved slowly, relentlessly. It caught Hook and held for a moment. Laurie took another step backward. Inexorably the light caught up with her and held.

Laurie reached for the knife at her side.

Then a woman's voice said, "What are you doing in my barn?"

Laurie was too relieved to speak. Perhaps the woman would have her arrested for trespassing, perhaps she would be turned over to the police and end up in an orphanage, but right at that moment there was no room in her for anything except relief that it was not the wayfaring stranger.

The woman stepped inside. She kept the light on Laurie so Laurie could not see her except as a vague outline. She came closer.

"Were you caught in the storm?" Her voice was unexpectedly gentle.

"Yes," Laurie said.

"Well, it was a bad one, and still is. I heard my peacocks scream so I came to see if they were all right. Then I saw your horse's tracks leading to the barn."

"Peacocks?" Laurie said.

"Yes. They make an ungodly racket. But they're so beautiful, I keep them anyway."

"I thought it was a person," Laurie said. "I was just going to see what the trouble was."

"You'd better come up to the house and dry out."

"I'm all right," Laurie said. "We were just going." Peacocks! She had never even seen a picture of a peacock. It was something as unknown as a llama or a Galápagos turtle, something you just read about.

"You're drenched to the skin," the woman said.

Laurie didn't want to go with her. There was no telling what it would lead to. "Really, I'm O.K.," she said.

"You're shaking like an aspen leaf. What about your horse? Should we do something to him?"

"He's fine." If only the woman would go away.

"Is he hungry?" She took a bucket off a shelf and filled it from a barrel. "I've got oats here just going to waste. My grand-niece was here last spring with her horse." She held out the bucket to Laurie. "You'll have to give it to him. I'm scared to death of horses."

Laurie took her bucket. "He's not too sure about strangers."

"Neither are you, I take it." The woman waited while Laurie gave Hook the oats. "Come on now, up to the house with you." She took Laurie's arm. It was still raining hard. She picked up the open umbrella that she had left outside and shook the rain off and held it over them. "You stay close to me so you won't get wet. Though I suppose you're soaked anyway."

"I had a poncho," Laurie said.

She stole a quick look at the woman beside her. She was not much taller than Laurie and rather slight. She had black hair, mostly covered by an old felt hat. Her eyes were dark brown and lively.

"You should have come up to the house," the woman said. "Heavens, anyone would be glad to shelter you in a storm like this." She stopped at a roofed enclosure and peered in. "There are my peacocks. They don't like the weather."

Laurie stared at them in amazement. She had never imagined any living thing being so brilliantly beautiful. The designs and the colors looked as if somebody had painted them on the feathers. She wondered if her grandfather would mind if she had a peacock of her own. He might not like that screaming.

"Shoo, Guinevere," the woman said to the peahen, who was not so brilliant as the males. "You, Lord Alfred, get out of that wet mud." Another bolt of lightning struck nearby, and the woman grabbed Laurie's arm and ran for the house.

They went up the back steps into the kitchen. Although she had seen pictures in magazines, Laurie had never believed that kitchens like the one she stepped into really existed. It had never occurred to her that real people lived in them, except perhaps millionaires. It was big and spotlessly clean, with a big white stove and a white sink and a lot of cabinets and things. There were beautiful red pots on the stove, and a pot of ivy hung near a window. Laurie looked at the clean, patterned floor.

"I'm getting your floor all muddy."

"It'll wash." The woman took off her raincoat. She was wearing gray flannel slacks and a blue shirt. She held out her hand for Laurie's jacket. "Let's clap you into a hot bath, first of all. We can't have you catching a cold."

It made Laurie uneasy to give up her jacket. What if she wanted to get away in a hurry? But she couldn't think of any polite way to refuse. She wondered if the other rooms were this big, and why anybody needed so much space.

Laurie continued shivering, partly from cold, but partly from nervousness. She let the woman lead her down a hall, up a flight of stairs, and into a pretty little bedroom with chintz curtains and matching bedspread. Laurie thought it was the prettiest room she had ever seen. There were framed photographs on the bureau, and on the wall there was a vivid painting that Laurie couldn't make head or tail of. Near the bed stood a small desk with books and pens and paper.

The woman was rummaging around in the closet. She threw a quilted bathrobe onto the bed and then a pair of blue jeans and a flannel shirt. "I don't know how they'll fit," she said, "but they're dry." She opened a door into a bathroom, went in and turned on the water in the tub. "There," she said. "When you're warm and dry, come on downstairs and we'll have lunch." At the door she turned back. "My name is Emily Kimball. Most people call me Miss Emily. That's what happens to you when you teach school for forty years; you become an institition-tution."

Laurie heard her grandfather's hated word, "institution", and shivered again. When Miss Emily had left her, she took off her soggy clothes and went into the bathroom. She had seen pictures of bathrooms too, in some of the magazines that Uncle Arthur usually left with them, but she had never expected to be in one like this. The walls were pale lavender and the cupboards and the splashboard around the tub were white. Big fluffy towels, white with a lavender monogram, hung on chromium rods. There was a shaggy lavender rug on the floor. It was luxury unimaginable.

The tub began to fill up. The hot water made a pleasant warm steam. Then she was faced with a sudden terrible thought. How did you shut off the water? At the cabin, water was dipped out of buckets. She leaned over the tub and turned one of the shining handles. The volume of water increased. Hastily she turned it off and tried another handle and suddenly water was pouring down on her head. She shut that off. It had to be the third handle. She tried it. To her immense relief the water stopped.

She put one foot into the water. It was hot, but it felt good. Gingerly she let herself all the way in. A bathtub seemed to her a rather treacherous thing, all slippery surfaces. But as she let herself slide down into the water, she decided it was worth the risk. She lay back and relaxed and felt the fatigue and the tension slide away.

What must it be like to live in a world where you could have a hot bath any time you wanted it? Whenever she had one at the cabin, it meant lugging up buckets full of water and heating them and dumping them into a galvanized tub that was barely big enough for her to get into with her legs all cramped up. There was never very much water, and it was always too hot or too cold. There was no pleasure in a bath at the cabin beyond the satisfaction of getting clean, but this, now . . . this was a joy in itself.

She picked up a round blue cake of soap and smelled of it. It smelled like flowers. It seemed too good to use. She used it though, lathering herself with increasing enthusiasm. It was good to feel really clean again and she realized she had not felt properly clean since she started on her trip.

She stayed in the tub a long time, looking around the room with pleasure. She wished she could take it with her. It was so pretty. She put out her finger and traced the frosted design in the glass door that half-concealed the tub, a door, she discovered, that would slide shut. She closed it and giggled. It was like being in a tiny little room.

She wondered if it would be acceptable if she washed her hair. It was sticky from rain and dust. Deciding to risk it, she scrubbed her head with the soap until it was sudsy. She thought about turning on that overhead thing to rinse it, but she was afraid something might go wrong. She turned the faucet, which she felt a little more sure of, and put her head under that until it was too hot to stand.

When she finally got out of the tub and put on the soft bathrobe and went into the bedroom, she discovered that her own clothes were gone. It alarmed her. Where had they gone? How could she ever get away if she didn't have her clothes? Maybe this woman intended to make her a prisoner until she could call the police. She didn't really believe that though. Miss Emily seemed nice. Still, one couldn't be sure.

She flicked the light switch a few times to watch the overhead light go on and off. It sure beat kerosene lamps. She got dressed in Miss Emily's clothes, which were just a little too big. She smoothed back her wet hair, wishing she had a proper haircut. She studied herself in the long mirror. She had never seen all of herself at once before and she was rather surprised to find that she was so tall. She examined her face, turning it this way and that. She did not care for it much. Her nose was too thin and there were too many freckles. Her mouth was too wide. Well, it was the only face she had, and she would have to put up with it. She went out of the room and stood at the top of the stairs, feeling timid about going down.

Then Miss Emily came into the hall and saw her. "Come on down," she said. "I'm just lighting the fire."

Laurie went downstairs and followed her into a big living room. It was a beautiful room. The furniture was dark shining wood. The long low sofa that faced the fireplace was the color of bing cherries. There were many-colored braided rugs on the polished floor. Outside the wind and the rain lashed the windows, but inside it was warm and quiet. She watched Miss Emily kneel in front of the fireplace, where she poked at the logs, struck a match and held it to the kindling. The fire blazed up.

"There," she said. "That will cheer things up. Do you feel better? Come sit down. You haven't told me your name."

"Laurie."

"Well, Laurie, where do you live?"

Now she had to be careful. Kind as Miss Emily seemed to be, Laurie knew that she would not have the same ideas as her grandfather. If she knew the truth, she might feel it her duty to report Laurie to the authorities.

"I live up north a ways," Laurie said.

"I used to teach up in the northern part of the state. What town?"

"No town. We live in the country."

"Oh, I see." Her keen dark eyes searched Laurie's face. "How do you happen to be way down here?"

Again Laurie hesitated. "I have to do an important errand for my family."

Miss Emily chuckled. "I ask too many questions. Always did. I get interested in people."

"That's all right," Laurie said. She hoped she hadn't seemed rude. This was a nice lady. She could put her in a class with Alec Begg, she thought, though of course she wasn't really sure yet.

"It's just that it doesn't seem quite safe for a child your age to be gallivanting around the country alone on a horse. Are you hungry?"

"Yes."

"Good. So am I. Do you want to stay here or do you

want to come into the kitchen while I fix lunch?"

"I'll come with you." Laurie thought it might be just as well to keep an eye on what was going on.

They went into the kitchen, and Miss Emily pulled out a stool for Laurie to sit on. She opened the tall white refrigerator, and Laurie saw neat rows of milk bottles and containers of food. It was certainly a lot easier to handle than Grandfather's well. But you had to pay a price for all this civilized stuff, she was sure of that, not just in money but in the way you lived. You'd probably have to live near a town, for instance. And what if the electricity failed to work? Then where would you be?

Miss Emily opened a compartment and took out some celery. She broke off a stalk, washed it, and gave it to Laurie. "That will tide you over till I get things ready."

Laurie bit into it hungrily. It was crisp. She loved celery but they seldom had it because it was hard to keep fresh.

Miss Emily dumped the contents of some frozen packages into two kettles and turned handles on the stove. Two little rings of fire lit up.

"How did you do that without a match?" Laurie said.

Miss Emily looked at her curiously. "Didn't you ever see a gas stove before?"

"No." She was sorry she had mentioned it. "Our stove burns wood," she explained. "I've seen gas stoves in magazines but I never knew how they worked."

"Well, the gas is piped into the stove from outside. There's a little pilot light here that burns all the time. When I turn the handle, the flame jumps over to this ring." She shook her head. "That's a terrible explanation. You can see I'm not a physics teacher."

"Where does the gas come from in the first place?" She wondered if her grandfather knew about this.

"Out of the ground originally. Then it's transported in big pipes across the country and piped to each person's house."

It was certainly a surprising world. In a little room beyond the kitchen another square white machine was making sloshing sounds. Miss Emily saw her look at it.

"I had to do some washing," she said, "so I tossed in your clothes, too. By the time you need them, they'll be clean and dry."

"How can they dry in this weather?" She hoped Miss Emily didn't think she was going to stay for days and days.

"I have a dryer."

That was a new one. Laurie had to see. She slid off the stool and went into the laundry. The washing machine had a glass porthole in front so she could see the suds swooshing around and the clothes whirling by. That other tall white thing must be the dryer. Electric, too? Boy, she thought, Ben Franklin really started something.

"I hope you'll like this stuff," Miss Emily said when Laurie came back into the kitchen. "I invented it."

Laurie watched her boil some frozen peas that looked like little green bullets, and then dump in some crabmeat and shrimp and something else that she couldn't identify at all, but the label on the can said "bean sprouts". Then Miss Emily put the whole business into a cream sauce. Laurie was so hungry she would have eaten anything, but she did wonder what in the world all that stuff dumped together was going to taste like.

The sudden shrill ringing of a bell made her jump.

Miss Emily took the receiver off a white telephone that hung on the wall. "Hello?" Then she smiled. "Yes, Sheriff, I'm all right."

Laurie grew stiff with alarm. Why was Miss Emily talking to the sheriff? Had she called him about Laurie while Laurie was taking her bath? Maybe the whole thing was a trap. She edged toward the door. If only she had her own clothes on. She wondered if they could arrest her if she ran away in somebody else's clothes. Her hand tightened on the door knob. Miss Emily gave her a rather puzzled look and Laurie waited to see what would happen.

chapter 9

Laurie listened tensely.

"No," Miss Emily was saying. "I couldn't see any place that it hit here. Everything seems to be all right." She listened. "Thank you for calling, Jeff." She hung up. "That was the sheriff," she said. "He used to be a student of mine, and he likes to look out for me. He was worried about that bolt of lightning." She went back to the stove.

Laurie relaxed. She would have to be careful though. This woman was a friend of the sheriff's.

"I guess it's ready," Miss Emily said. "You drink milk, don't you?"

"I love milk," Laurie said.

Miss Emily got a folded table from the laundry room

and said, "Will you set this card table up in front of the fireplace? It's cozier there."

Laurie took it into the living room. Set it up? What did you do with it? She studied it from all angles. Finally she tugged at one of the legs, and it came out into place. She felt quite proud of herself when she had the table standing on all four legs.

The fire felt warm and good, but Laurie kept an eye out the window in case that sheriff showed up. Miss Emily might have been telling her a story.

Miss Emily brought in a tablecloth and silver and then a tray with two plates, a glass of milk, and a cup of tea.

"There," she said. "We can eat."

Laurie took her first bite with some suspicion, but the food was delicious; and although she tried not to eat too fast, she finished long before Miss Emily.

"Let me get you some more," Miss Emily said. "I like to see people eat."

"I can get it." It made Laurie uneasy to have Miss Emily wait on her. She jumped up and bumped the table with her knee and spilled some of Miss Emily's tea. "Oh, I'm sorry . . ." She was so clumsy! It was a good thing she didn't live around other people because she would always be doing the wrong thing.

"That's nothing," Miss Emily said. She mopped up the tea with a paper napkin. "When I was your age, I used to knock over my glass of milk so regularly that my mother brought a dish towel to the table with her, just to be ready. 'Here comes the milk train,' my father would say."

When Laurie came back with her filled plate, Miss Emily said, "What grade are you in, Laurie?"

"Eighth." Long ago she had figured out just what

grade she would be in from year to year, although she sometimes finished her correspondence work ahead of a regular year. Pretty soon now, she was going to have to go to a real high school. She didn't like the idea, but her grandfather said she had to. "You can't grow up ignorant," he said. "Your mama and daddy would never forgive me."

"I taught high school English," Miss Emily was saying. "I retired last year."

"Did you like to be a teacher?"

"Sometimes it's wonderful and sometimes it's so frustrating you can hardly stand it. You want to do so much, and you can't do a tenth of it." She sipped her tea. "Would you like to teach?"

"Oh, no," Laurie said. "I wouldn't want to get mixed up with all those people."

"You don't trust people much, do you?"

Laurie shook her head.

"You'll learn to though. Time and again they'll let you down, but by and large you have to trust them."

"They can wreck you," Laurie said, quoting her grandfather.

"Yes, they can. It's a chance you have to take."

Laurie thought about what she had said. She wondered who was right.

"That young man, the sheriff, for instance," Miss Emily said. "When he came to me, he was a real hellion. But I thought he had some good in him, and I took a chance with him. Now everybody relies on him to protect them. Not that I can claim all the credit for Jeff Parsons, of course." She cleared the dishes and brought in two big pieces of strawberry pie with whipped cream.

"I wish I could cook like you," Laurie said.

"All cooking consists of is following the recipe and giving a darn about how it comes out."

When lunch was over, Miss Emily said, "I usually take a nap about now. I feel my age after lunch. Would you mind if I left you to yourself?"

"Of course not," Laurie said.

"Anything special you'd like to do?"

Laurie had noticed a little room off the hall that was lined with books. "Could I look at your books?"

Miss Emily looked pleased. "Of course." She took Laurie into the little room. Three of the walls were filled with bookshelves from floor to ceiling. At the fourth wall there was a small desk and a window. The room also held a comfortable-looking chair and a footstool.

"I wish I had all those books," Laurie said.

"A teacher accumulates a lot of books."

Impulsively Laurie said, "My father was a teacher. I have his books."

Miss Emily looked at her. "Was?"

"He died a long time ago."

"Do you live with your mother then?"

The trouble with saying one thing was that it led to another. Now she had gotten into more than she had intended. But she couldn't lie.

"No, she died, too. In an accident. I live with my grandfather."

"Oh. Well, you're lucky to have a grandfather you can live with."

Laurie was glad she said that instead of saying she was unlucky not to have parents.

Miss Emily gestured toward the books. "Enjoy yourself."

When she had gone, Laurie looked outdoors. It was still raining hard and there was a strong wind that slashed branches against the window. The box elders in Miss Emily's yard heaved and swayed as if they were doing some clumsy dance. Laurie was concerned about the weather. She ought to be getting on her way, but this was no weather for travel. She looked around the room. There was something that she realized after a moment must be a television set. She hoped Miss Emily would turn it on later. She had always wanted to see one. Her grandfather had seen one when he had stopped for a whiskey at the bar in town, and he had told her about it. It was hard to believe.

She looked at the books. There were so many. Finally

she took down Thomas Hardy's *The Mayor of Caster-bridge*. She had read *Jude the Obscure* and liked it. She settled down in the comfortable chair. Out in the hall a grandfather's clock chimed the hour.

The book was so interesting it seemed no time at all before Miss Emily reappeared. She had changed into a full blue skirt with white flowers on it and a white blouse, her black hair combed back smoothly into a knot. She looked at the book. "How do you like it?"

"It's good," Laurie said.

"Hardy is good."

"That man, though, the mayor. He does such bad things, and yet you feel sorry for him."

Miss Emily shrugged. "We're all part bad and part good."

That was a new idea to Laurie. It was one she needed some time to think about.

Dinner that night was so good she hated to have it end. Tender juicy steaks, baked potatoes with sour cream and chives, fresh lima beans, and a salad. She ate and ate.

After dinner Miss Emily said, "Would you like to look at the television? It gets worse every day, but I like to watch the news."

Laurie sat on the edge of the footstool expectantly while Miss Emily twirled dials. Finally the picture appeared. Laurie was amazed at its clarity. It was an animal film about a man who had gone to the South Pole to study penguins. Laurie was fascinated. She couldn't understand how it could possibly work.

When the film was over, the news came on. Laurie listened to every word although she didn't understand all that the man was saying. Then he showed some pictures of a street riot. It was horrifying. Police and men and boys were fighting ferociously, slugging each other, brutally dragging people and beating them. Laurie couldn't believe it.

"Is it real?" she said. "Is it happening?"

"It is," Miss Emily said grimly.

Then her grandfather was right; the world was as bad as he said, or worse. He had never described anything as bad as this. The people in the crowd seemed to be insane. She found herself shivering.

Abruptly Miss Emily got up and turned it off. She looked upset. "Violence and violence and violence," she said. "Where will it all end?"

Laurie still felt shaky. "Is there much of that?"

"Too much. Too much." She got up and walked around the room, took down a book absently and put it back again. "And yet there *are* good things we are getting closer to. But the fight is so bloody." She sat down again. She looked tired. "It makes me feel old, and I hate feeling old."

"I'm not going to get mixed up in any mess like that," Laurie said. "I'm going to stay clear out of it."

Miss Emily shook her head. "It's our world and we're stuck with it." She looked at Laurie and smiled. "And it's not all bad, not by a long shot."

But Laurie felt sick to the very pit of her stomach. She could not forget those contorted brutal faces. "I don't want it," she said. "I'm going to stay out of it."

chapter 10

Laurie still felt shaken when she went to bed. Just when she had begun to hope that Miss Emily was right about there being good in the world, she had seen that awful riot. She wanted to go right to sleep and forget it. After her nights of sleeping on the ground, the bed was as comfortable as air, but she could not get to sleep. The pictures on the television screen kept flashing through her mind.

She turned on the bed lamp and got up. There were some books on Miss Emily's desk. She picked up a slim volume of poetry by Sylvia Plath. She got back into bed with it.

She was used to reading poetry, but she found some of

these hard going. Still, right in the midst of confusion about what the poet meant, she would come on a line that took her breath away. She kept on reading. Then she came to one stuck between the pages of the book, cut from a magazine, that made her sit up straight. She read it over again and then again, not exactly sure what it meant but excited by it in the same way that "Much Have I Travel'd in the Realms of Gold" and Amy Lowell's "Patterns" had excited her. She got up and found a pencil and a piece of paper on the desk and copied out the poem, writing carefully.

On the stiff twig up there
Bunches a wet black rook
Arranging and rearranging
　its feathers in the rain.

She wrote on, slowly, careful to get every word right. Then she came to the last lines and she read them over again before she wrote them down.

. . . . I only know that a rook
Ordering its black feathers can so shine
As to seize my senses, haul
My eyelids up, and grant
A brief respite from fear
Of total neutrality. With luck
Trekking stubborn through this season
Of fatigue, I shall
Patch together a content

Of sorts. Miracles occur,
If you care to call those spasmodic

84

Tricks of radiance miracles. The wait's
  begun again,

The long wait for the angel,
For that rare, random descent.

It made her want to cry, though she was not sure why.
A rook, as far as she knew, she had never seen, but a
mountain jay in the rain . . . it was just the way the
poem said.

She would have to make enough money to buy some
new books. If things like this were being written, she
wanted to know about it. She would ask Uncle Arthur
about the smoked fish and meat idea.

She turned out the light beside her bed and lay back on
the pillow, thinking about how beautiful the world was
and wondering why its beauty should make you ache.

Later in the night she had a nightmare. In it she
dreamed that she was in Miss Emily's classroom, which
looked like Miss Emily's kitchen. Miss Emily was teach-
ing her to do fractions. And suddenly a horde of giants
poured into the room, tremendous creatures each with
one eye in the center of his forehead. Behind them an
angel hovered, but they blocked him from her sight.
They began to beat Miss Emily and they had grabbed
her, Laurie, when she awoke sobbing with terror.

At first she could not remember where she was. She
could hear music playing softly in the background. Then
Miss Emily was standing beside her in a nightgown and
robe.

"What is it, Laurie?" she said. She put her hand on
Laurie's forehead. "Did you have a bad dream?"

Laurie sat up. She was trembling. "Yes. A terrible dream."

"Why don't you come downstairs and have a glass of milk with me?" Miss Emily said. "I was just going down." She handed Laurie her robe.

When they went past Miss Emily's bedroom, the music grew more distinct. Laurie stopped.

"I hope that didn't disturb you," Miss Emily said. "Sometimes I don't sleep too well and it soothes me to listen to music."

The music soared and fell and soared again, a cascade of sound like a waterfall. Laurie had never heard anything like it. She listened intently. It made her want to stand up on tiptoe and fling out her arms. It banished the terror of her dream. "It's beautiful," she said.

"It's Mahler's Fifth. I'll turn it up so we can hear it downstairs." She went into the bedroom and turned a knob on the record player. The music filled the house.

"I didn't know there was music like that," Laurie said.

She went downstairs behind Miss Emily, listening and listening. In the kitchen Miss Emily poured two glasses of milk and set out a plate of sugar cookies. Laurie found that she was hungry.

"What was your dream about?" Miss Emily said.

Laurie told her.

"I'm sorry you saw all that violence on TV." She was silent for a few minutes. Then she said, "When I was young, all sorts of things used to upset me terribly. I was especially afraid that something awful was going to happen to the people I loved. It was a daily and nightly horror. Then I decided I had to do something before I became a nervous wreck. I undertook to change my attitude. It wasn't easy, but I finally made it." She paused. "You see, for one thing, the things you dread are seldom the things that happen, so you can't prepare yourself in any specific way for disaster. And you can't, you just can't, live out your life in fear and dread . . . or suspicion. The world is a hard place—your grandfather is right if he has taught you that—but it is also a wonderful place. Music and art and books and lovely places and most of all, people."

"People are mean," Laurie said.

"Lots of them are, but lots more will make you weep with their kindness and generosity."

Laurie thought for a minute. Miss Emily had seen more of the world than she had.

"Well," she said, "thanks for talking to me. I'll remember what you said."

Miss Emily laughed. "No, you won't. But that's all right." She studied Laurie's face. "I wish I knew more about you."

Laurie was tempted to tell her, all about her journey and Grandfather and the Saturday Mine, about being a property owner and all that. But she had promised Grandfather to be careful.

"When it's all over," she said, "I'll write you a long letter."

"I would like that," Miss Emily said. "And Laurie, any time you feel like coming to visit me, I would like to have you. Will you remember that?"

"Yes, I will," Laurie said. "And I'll come, too, by jingo." She glanced into the laundry and saw her jeans and shirt clean and pressed. "You didn't have to press them," she said.

"It only took a minute," Miss Emily said. "By the way, I took the things out of your jeans pockets and put them in your bureau drawer."

My bureau drawer, Laurie thought. Miss Emily had a nice way of making her feel as if she belonged there. She jumped, at a scratching sound on the back door.

"What's that?"

"There's a member of my family you haven't met." Miss Emily went to the door.

Laurie stiffened. She didn't want to meet anyone. And who would come at this hour?

Miss Emily opened the door and a handsome black cat with green eyes bounded into the kitchen. Laurie let out her breath in relief. "A cat."

"This is Mistress Quickly," Miss Emily said, rubbing the cat's ears. "She has been gone two days, heaven knows where. I don't ask her her business and she doesn't ask me mine." She got a can of cat food from the closet and emptied it into an aluminum dish. The cat ate hungrily. When she was through, she jumped into Miss Emily's lap, purring.

"I had better send you back to bed," Miss Emily said. "You need your sleep."

"It's stopped raining," Laurie said.

"So I suppose in the morning you'll take off for parts unknown. You know, I have that little car sitting there in the barn. It never gets enough exercise. You could leave your horse here, and I could drive you where it is you must go."

It was tempting. But Laurie was sure that if Miss Emily knew how far she was going, she would not offer to drive her, and she would probably try to stop her. She shook her head.

"Thanks just the same. I'm beholden to you."

"You are stubborn as a mule," Miss Emily said. "You will probably achieve every goal you set out for, all your life."

"So far I don't have any goals," she said. Miss Emily's use of the word "mule" made her think of the singing stranger. For a little while she had forgotten him. She wished with all her heart that she could tell Miss Emily the whole story.

Miss Emily slung the cat over her shoulder and walked to the foot of the stairs with Laurie. "Will the music keep you awake?"

"No, I like it." Laurie patted the cat, said good night to Miss Emily, and went up to bed. For a while she lay listening to the music. It rolled her along; she felt like a chip of wood being carried on a strong current. She wondered about record players. Did you need electricity to make them work? She'd like to have one. She thought about everything that had happened to her since she left home. It was a confusing succession of things that didn't seem to add up to any answers. She thought about the things Miss Emily had said, and she thought about the riot on television, and she thought about the poem about the rook. And finally she came back to just listening to the music again. At last she fell asleep.

chapter 11

Laurie woke early, but she could already hear Miss
Emily moving around downstairs. She wondered when
she ever slept. She got up, took a quick bath, and went
back into the bedroom to find her own clothes neatly
laid over the back of a chair. She got her wallet and the
folded map from the bureau drawer and went down to
the kitchen, following the good smells of breakfast cooking.

"Good morning," Miss Emily said. She was frying
bacon and the delicious smell of it made Laurie's nose
crinkle.

"Good morning," Laurie said.

Miss Emily had set two places at the kitchen table. "Sit

down and have your orange juice. I've already had mine."

Laurie drank the cold orange juice slowly. Miss Emily put two plates on the table with bacon and eggs and toast. She poured coffee for herself and milk for Laurie.

"I brought your pack in from the barn," she said, "and I put a few things in it that you might be needing."

Laurie's pack sat by the door. It was bulging.

"You are awful good to me," Laurie said.

"I'm a natural-born mother hen, always fussing over people. If you had to put up with me very long, you'd go crazy."

"No, I like it," Laurie said. She was not used to being taken care of, and she had not known till now that she missed it. Grandfather looked after the main things of course, but there were all these little things that maybe just women thought of.

After breakfast they walked to the barn. Laurie felt sad about going. She did not want to leave Miss Emily and this place.

Miss Emily stooped over and picked up a peacock feather. She put it in Laurie's hand.

"When you get to thinking the world is hopeless," she said, "look at that."

Laurie looked at the metallic-bright colors of the circles on the feather. She smoothed it out carefully and put it in her pocket.

Hook nickered happily when he saw her. She led him outside. It was a clear sparkling day after the rain. Laurie felt the cool air wash down her arms like water. But the rain and wind and hail had knocked many leaves off the trees, and a few branches lay strewn about the yard.

"Look at my aspen," Miss Emily said. "They look more like November than July."

After Laurie got into the saddle, she looked down at Miss Emily. "I don't know what to say," she said. "How can I tell you . . ."

"Just take care of yourself," Miss Emily said briskly. "And come back and see me some time if you feel like it. But only if you really feel like it, mind."

"I will come," Laurie said.

Miss Emily smiled at her but her eyes brightened with tears, and Laurie realized with a shock of surprise that Miss Emily was lonely.

"I'll be careful, and I'll come back. I'll probably come back so often, you'll get sick of seeing me." She turned Hook's head and rode away quickly. She was afraid she was going to cry, too. She felt as if she were leaving a part of herself again. That image of herself in the long mirror—was it still there?

She went back down the road she had come until she could turn off into the forest again, where she checked her compass to make sure she was on the right track. It was a beautiful morning, and she began to enjoy it. She stopped once to look at three elk who were grazing in a little clearing. They lifted their antlered heads and watched her curiously. She hoped no hunter would find them in the fall.

When the sun was overhead, she stopped for lunch. There was a narrow rushing creek and big pines that came close to the water's edge. She and Hook drank from the creek, and she splashed water over her face.

Anxious to see what Miss Emily had put in the pack, she took out two cans of tuna fish, a can of Spam, a can of crabmeat, a package of mashed potato mix, a can of cocoa mix, a carefully wrapped package of cookies, and some lump sugar for Hook. At the bottom of the pack on top of her change of clothes was a dark blue pull-over sweater and a note. In the note Miss Emily said, "Laurie, you may need this sweater. I don't want you getting sopping wet and not having something dry to put on. If you come back to see me, you can return it. If not, don't worry about it. Happy Journey. Miss Emily." And she had added her address and telephone number.

Laurie put her cheek against the sweater. It was soft and woolly. Carefully she put it back in the pack and looked at the array of food. What to have for lunch? Finally deciding on tuna fish, she pulled out the can opener on her knife and opened the can. She ate it hungrily and then had a few cookies. Finally she gave Hook a lump of sugar, packed up her things, and started off again.

A strong wind came up in the early afternoon. It moaned through the trees and whipped their branches. She had to be careful not to be struck by the limbs of the trees.

The trail came out of the woods, and she rode for a while alongside pastures that were fenced in. There was a herd of black Angus, oblivious of the wind, munching grass. Far off across the pasture two horses ran with flying manes. She could see the chimney of a house down in a little hollow. There were frequent large "No Trespassing" signs along the barbed wire fence.

She was riding along with her head down against the wind when she heard a horse's scream. Just ahead of her a young colt was caught in the barbed wire, pulling frantically and screaming with pain. She could see the blood on his chest where the wire had gashed him. A mare stood close to him, whinnying and tossing her head, and pacing nervously around him.

Laurie slid to the ground and ran to the fence. The wind almost knocked her over. It howled, and the colt screamed. She tried to release him from her side of the fence, but she couldn't get at him. He just pulled harder and cut himself worse. She separated the strands of wire and let herself into the pasture. The mare whinneyed and hovered close, anxious.

"Boy, you're really tangled up," Laurie said. The colt kicked at her. "Hey, cut that out. I'm trying to help you." But he was too terrified to be soothed. His flanks were cut too and when she tried to get her arm around him to hold him still, she got blood all over her hands. "Just hold still," she said to him. "Doggone it, I can't get you loose if you don't hold still."

He jerked his head around and bit her arm.

"Ouch!" she said. "Cut that out." She had him almost freed now. Then she heard a shout. It was just barely audible, in the wind. She turned her head to look. Far away on the other side of the pasture, so far that he looked tiny, she saw a man. He was waving his arm and yelling.

"He doesn't want me in his pasture," she said to the colt. "But I'll have you loose in a second." She waved her arm at the man and tried to shout to him that his colt was caught in the fence, but the wind tossed her words away. "He'll just have to get mad, I guess," she said. She bent her head over the colt. He was almost loose now. Just one strand of wire was caught around his foreleg.

Something whizzed past her and plopped in the soft wood of the fence post. She looked at it in astonishment. "Good grief, the guy is shooting at me!" She stood up and waved her free arm at the man again and shouted, "Your colt is caught." To the colt she said, "He thinks I'm stealing you."

She got the colt's leg loose. He staggered backward, then caught his balance and ran in a frenzied circle around his mother.

Laurie felt a hot pain in her upper left arm. She ran for the loose place in the fence and let herself through, aware of the warm blood on her arm. She caught Hook and scrambled into the saddle, put her head down, and rode.

When she was out of sight of the pasture, she slowed Hook. She felt faint and her arm burned.

"Well," she said to Hook, "I'm shot. What do we do now?" The man must have had a high-powered rifle with a scope to get her from that distance. Uncle Arthur had one of those guns so she had seen them, but she had never expected to be shot by one.

She pulled up her sleeve gingerly and looked at her arm. It was still bleeding rather badly. She dismounted to see what she could do about it. She took her arm out of the sleeve, wincing with pain, and used some water from her canteen to try to wash the wound. Was the bullet still in there? She tore the sleeve out of her shirt and used it as a bandage. It was awkward trying to bandage her own arm, but she managed a makeshift affair. All that blood made her feel sick, and her arm throbbed and burned. She sat down with her back to a yellow pine.

She wished she was in Miss Emily's comfortable bed. She knew she ought to get up and do something but she couldn't decide what, so she just sat still. The wind made little whirlpools of the pine needles and blew dust in her face and howled through the trees.

"Oh, be still," she said. "Can't you be quiet while I think?"

She sat very still hoping the pain would go away. But it didn't. A gray squirrel scampered up and down the trunk of the pine, peering at her curiously with his bright eyes. Once he jumped to the ground and sat on his hind legs beside her boot, his nose twitching and his tail weaving.

"What would you do in a fix like this?" Laurie said to him.

He took alarm and ran up the tree again.

She looked at Hook. "I guess we'd better stay here for the night. I don't feel too good." She made herself get up and unsaddle him and hitch him to a nearby tree. "I'm sorry there's no creek. It's not a very good place to camp, but I can't go any further right now." She gave him one of Miss Emily's lumps of sugar. Oh, Miss Emily, she thought, and her eyes filled with tears.

But there was no good in feeling sorry for herself. She threw the blanket onto the pine needles and tried to find a comfortable position to lie down in. She couldn't sleep; her arm hurt too much. Besides, it was still day. She just lay still and stared at the scudding clouds in the sky. Eventually she dozed a little, but every time she moved, the pain in her arm brought her sharply awake. Once her grandfather had been shot in the leg by a trigger-happy hunter and he had had to go to the doctor and have the bullet taken out.

It upset her to think that that rancher had shot at her

without even finding out who she was or what she was doing. If God gave us the power to reason, why did he make it so tough to use it? She wished that life could be clear and patterned, and then you would know what to expect next. The way it was, you just never knew.

She was worried about Hook because he was hitched where there were only pine needles and he couldn't graze. After thinking about it and bracing herself for it for twenty minutes or so, she finally got to her feet and set out to find a place where he could graze. At first there was nothing, but then quite unexpectedly she came upon an opening in the trees. There was grass, and even better, there was a stream. It was only about a foot wide, but it was water.

She went back and got her blanket and saddle and led Hook to the grassy place. At once he began to eat. Dizzy, she sank to the ground. When she felt a little better, she took off her blood-stained shirt and tried to rinse it out in the stream, hanging it on a bush to dry. Then with one hand she rummaged in the pack until she found her clean shirt. She put it on, leaving the left sleeve hanging free. She checked the bandage. It was blood-stained, but she thought the bleeding had stopped. She was thirsty. It was difficult to lie on her stomach and drink from the creek as she would usually do, so she filled the canteen and drank from that. I ought to be boiling this water, she thought; it isn't safe to drink water this close to towns. But she didn't have the strength to build a fire and boil the water. She drank almost a canteen-full.

Finally she fell asleep, but she woke up half an hour later when she turned over on her wounded arm. She felt it bleeding again. She was going to have to do something about it in the morning.

She didn't feel like eating, but she mixed some of the cocoa with cold water and drank that. It didn't mix very well and she got a big lump of chocolate in her mouth when she came to the bottom of the cup. But it seemed to make her feel a little better. She decided to eat a can of tuna fish.

It was ten o'clock before darkness came. She grew restless and bored waiting for sleep and began reciting poetry aloud to pass the time. She went through Shelley's "Ozymandias" and Keats' "Ode to Autumn," although she couldn't remember all of that. Then she did Milton's "On His Blindness". "We also serve who only stand and wait," she said. She stopped to think about Milton and his blindness. What patience he must have had to be able to put up with it and to write a poem like that. She began it again. "When I consider how my light is spent, Ere half my days in this dark world and wide, And that one talent which is death to hide, Lodged with me useless . . ." She had never stopped to think much about how he must have felt. Now she felt like crying for poor Mr. Milton. But suddenly she realized that he didn't need her to cry for him; he had managed all right. Miss Emily was right, some people had a courage that made you tingle. Maybe that was what kept the human race going.

chapter 12

She had a bad night. The pain in her arm kept her from sleeping much, and when she did fall asleep she had bad dreams. Once a big animal crashed through the woods very close to her and she was afraid a bear might have smelled her food, but whatever it was went away again.

She got hungry in the middle of the night and opened the first can she could find in the dark. It was the crab-meat. She ate it and a couple of cookies and then she was terribly thirsty. The canteen was empty. She got up with a groan and went down to the creek and drank thirstily. As she started to go, a movement on the other side of the stream made her look up. A doe was watching her. They stood for a moment looking at each other in the dim light. Then the doe bent her head and drank and disappeared into the woods.

Laurie was glad when daylight came. Her arm felt hot and stiff and it throbbed. She didn't bother about breakfast. It was hard to get into the saddle, but she managed it finally and rode slowly toward what she hoped was the highway.

The sun glared down at her like a baleful red eye. The mosquitoes bothered her. She would have to spend some of her money for fly dope. She felt weak and dizzy. For once she hoped that a town was not far away. Sometimes the highway ran for miles through empty countryside.

The sun climbed higher, and no air stirred. She slapped at the mosquitoes, but there were always more. The flies were bothering Hook. He rippled his skin and swished his tail and tossed his head impatiently. Once Laurie dozed and almost slipped from the saddle.

She sat up straight, forcing herself awake, nudging Hook into a trot. It hurt her arm almost unbearably, but she had to get somewhere. She was afraid she would pass out.

She came at last to the highway. There was no town there, but as she came down the road and rounded a curve, she saw a settlement.

It was not much of a place—a little restaurant, which was open, and three or four stores, and a gas station. She dismounted awkwardly, tied Hook to the old hitching rail that was still standing, and went into the restaurant. It was empty except for the man behind the counter. He was a big tough-looking man.

"Hi," he said.

"Hello," Laurie said. "Do you happen to know where

I can find a doctor?" Her voice sounded hoarse.

The man glanced at her bandaged arm. "We haven't got no regular doctor. Doc Ashe retired last year."

"Oh," she said. She would have to keep on going then. She wasn't sure that she could.

"Doc Ashe still goes out for emergencies though," he said. "He's still got his office across the street for when people are bad off." The man studied her for a minute. She was leaning against the counter in an effort not to fall. "I could call him for you."

"I'd sure appreciate it," Laurie said.

The man took the receiver down from a wall phone and dialed a number. Then he said, "Doc? This is Vince, over to the restaurant. Hope I didn't get you out of bed. . . . Well, there's a kid here wants to see you. Hurt her arm some way. She looks kind of green around the gills. . . . Yeah. O.K." He hung up. "He'll be right down." He poured a cup of coffee and slid it across the counter toward her.

"Thanks," Laurie said. "How much is it?"

"That's all right."

"No, I want to pay for it." Don't be beholden to people, her grandfather always told her.

He shrugged. "It's a dime."

She got the dime out of her pocket and gave it to him. She didn't often drink coffee, but this morning she needed it. She sipped it and it burned her tongue. She waited a minute and tried again. The hotness felt good in her stomach.

Vince busied himself cleaning out the coffee maker and starting a new batch of coffee. He did not talk. She was grateful to him for not asking questions.

He squinted out through the plate-glass window. "The doc just drove up."

"Thanks," Laurie said.

"Forget it."

She slid down from the stool and went across the street. The doctor, unlocking the office door, gave her a quick searching glance and nodded. "Come on in."

The office was cool and dark. He switched on an overhead light, put the black bag he was carrying on his desk, and turned to her. "What's the trouble?"

"Somebody shot me."

"Shot you!" He gently unwrapped the bloody bandage. The dried blood made it stick and it hurt. "Just one little place here," he said, "and we'll have it."

Laurie turned her head so she wouldn't have to look at her arm. The doctor bent over it, poking it gently here and there. It hurt but she gritted her teeth and hung onto the edge of the desk with her other hand.

"The bullet went through," he said. "Just a superficial wound. But we'll have to clean it out. Now . . ." He leaned back against the desk and looked at her. "I have to get your parents' permission to do this."

Laurie's heart sank. Why couldn't he just get it over with?

"My parents are dead," she said.

"Who is responsible for you?"

"My grandfather."

He picked up a pad of paper. "Well, give me his name and phone number and I'll call him. He doesn't know about this, I gather?"

She shook her head. "You can't call him. We live way up north in the woods. There's no phone."

"Any near neighbors?"

"No neighbors at all."

He made a little gesture of exasperation. "You folks who live the simple life can really complicate things." He thought for a minute. Then he picked up the phone and dialled. "Harvey," he said, "I got a problem. There's a kid here that got shot in the arm. I've got to clean that wound out or she'll be in trouble. She lives with her grandfather way to hell and gone up in the woods, and there's no way to reach him. I'm going to clean out that wound." He listened for a moment, and then he grinned. "You can take my license away from me if you want to. Then maybe I'll get a little peace and quiet. . . . No, I don't know yet what happened. I'll give you a report . . . Thanks, Harvey." He hung up. "All right," he said to Laurie, "climb up on that operating table and we'll break a few laws." He lit a sterilizer and put some instruments in it.

Laurie looked at the table suspiciously. She didn't want to lie down on it.

"Go on, lie down," he said. "No need to be skittish." When she lay down, he covered all of her except her arm with a white sheet. He filled a long needle and came up to her. She flattened against the table.

"Ever have a shot?" he said.

"No."

"It will sting for a second, then it's all over. It will keep you from feeling pain when I clean out the wound." He swabbed her arm with a piece of wet cotton. Laurie held her breath. She felt the light quick sting of the needle and then a longer smarting as he pushed the plunger. Then he pulled it out.

"Just lie still for a few minutes." He went to the other side of the room and busied himself with instruments. "I'm spoiled," he said. "When I was in regular practice, my nurse did all this."

Laurie felt drowsy. Gradually the pain in her arm began to subside. He came back and gave her another shot, but she didn't feel that one.

"Close your eyes and take it easy," he said. "The worst is over."

She felt sleepy. "Did you clean it?"

"No, but you won't feel it when I do. You may be aware of my poking at your arm, but it won't hurt." His voice sounded far away.

She closed her eyes. Then time seemed to do odd things. It seemed hours later that she felt a pressure on her arm. Something was going on. It frightened her at first, but it didn't hurt so she relaxed. Then when she opened her eyes again, the doctor was sitting at his desk writing.

She looked at her arm. It was neatly bandaged and in a sling. "Can I go now?" she said.

"I have to ask you a few questions first. And then I want you to rest for a little while." He pulled a chair up beside her. "First of all, what's your name?" He waited and when she didn't answer he said, "I have to make out a report for the police when there's a gunshot wound."

The police. She was in for it now. But she didn't see any way out. She couldn't make up a story for the police. If they found out she had lied, it would really go hard on her.

"Laurie James," she said.

"Address?"

"Hawkins Dry Diggings, Montana."

He looked up. "Is there really such a place?"

"Yes."

He raised his eyebrows, but he wrote it down. "What is your grandfather's name?"

"Do I have to tell you?" she said. "He hates to get mixed up in things."

"It's just routine," he said. "Nobody will bother him."

"Peter Bent." Hoping it might help, she added, "We're property owners. We own a gold mine."

"I wish I did," the doctor said. "Now, how did you get shot?"

She told him the story.

He frowned. "Could you see what the man looked like?"

"No. He was way off. He must have had a scope."

He tapped his teeth with the end of the pen. "Was it a big pasture up northeast of here, with woods and a hill on the other side?"

"That sounds like it," she said.

"I thought so." He looked angry. "Cy Willoughby," he said. "If I wasn't in the presence of a young lady, I'd have a few choice things to say about Cy Willoughby. He's pulled this kind of stunt before. He used to fire buckshot at anybody that came near his place, and then he got himself a high-powered rifle. He probably didn't mean to hit you, but the fact is he did hit you. When you're feeling better, you should go on down to the police station and bring charges against him."

"Oh no," she said, startled. "I couldn't do that."

"Why not? He might have killed you. It's time somebody did something about him."

"But I was on his place. He probably thought I was trying to steal the colt."

"That's no reason to shoot a person."

"I can't go to the police," she said. "I couldn't do that."

"You aren't running away from home, are you?"

"Oh, no. Honestly, I'm not."

"Then why are you so leery of the police?"

"I just don't want to get mixed up with the law," she said. It was her grandfather's phrase.

Dr. Ashe laughed. "You sound like a character in a TV western. Your grandfather isn't a moonshiner or something, is he?"

"Of course not," she said. "I told you, he's a miner."

"O.K. Well, I want you to lie here for about half an hour. There's some shock involved in a thing like this, and you've lost quite a bit of blood. You aren't going to feel too hot for a while."

"I feel fine," she said. She started to sit up. "I could go now all right."

Firmly he pushed her back down. "Listen to me, Laurie James. I admire self-reliance and independence. But they can be carried too far. Common sense is also important. Don't be so all-fired independent that you can't accept help or advice from other people. We all need each other now and then."

"I asked you for help," she said.

"That's right, you did, and that was smart." He poured some tablets out of a big bottle into an envelope. "Take two of these, four hours apart, for pain. They may make you a little sleepy. And I want to see that arm day after tomorrow. Nine o'clock all right?"

She didn't know what to say, but he didn't wait for an answer. "I'd stay here with you but I promised to look in on a lady who's about to have a baby."

"I thought you were retired," Laurie said.

"Nobody believes it but me." He put on his jacket and packed up his black bag. "You just lie here like I told you, for about thirty minutes."

"How much money do I owe you?" Laurie said.

"You can pay me next time."

"I'd like to pay you now. How much is it, please?"

He came over and looked down at her. "You don't intend to come back, do you?"

She felt bad. He had been good to her. "I can't," she

said. "There's somewhere I have to get to."

He shook his head. "Promise me you'll see another doctor then," he said.

"I'll try."

"Try isn't good enough. You promise."

"All right." She felt too weak to argue. As he turned to go, she said, "You didn't say how much I owe you."

"Well, let's see," he said. "Let's say for a gunshot wound incurred by a little girl through no fault of her own, one dollar."

"Are you sure that's all?"

"One dollar."

She got her wallet out of her pocket and took out one of the silver dollars and gave it to him. He turned it over in his hand.

"These are valuable," he said. "I know where I can get at least $1.85 for it. So I owe you eighty-five cents." He took the change out of his pocket and gave it to her. "All right, Laurie, you take care of yourself." He nodded and went out.

She heard the front door close and then the engine of his car start up. She lay still, feeling weak. Suddenly she wondered if he had gone to the police with the report he had made out. If he had, they would be swarming all over her asking questions. She made herself get up, feeling very shaky. She looked on the desk. The report was still there. Then she felt ashamed of having suspected him. He had been kind and she wished she could have told him more of the truth; but like Miss Emily, he was friendly with the police. She was not going to end up in any orphanage, nor was she going to see Grandfather in any old folks' home, not after she had come this far.

She walked unsteadily to the door. She felt awful, but she had to get going. The police knew she was there, and they might just come on by to check up anyway. When she got out on the street, she stood indecisively for a moment. There was nobody around, but right in front of her was a glass-enclosed telephone booth. She looked at it for a long moment and then made a decision. In spite of what Grandfather had said about the telephone, this was an emergency. She was going to call up Uncle Arthur and tell him that she didn't think she could make it to Butte. Perhaps he could come and get her, and then they could go get Grandfather.

She glanced at Hook. He was contentedly munching weeds where she had hitched him. As she walked to the phone booth, her knees almost gave out. She went inside the booth. Now what? There was a book dangling from a chain. She put it up on the metal shelf and opened it. It was hard to do things with one arm in a sling. She opened the pages of the book. The telephone company certainly had a lot to say. It told you how to call the police, the highway patrol, the fire company, the doctor, the ambulance, and Information. Information might be what she needed. She read through all the business about area codes and how you shouldn't dig up telephone cable and what to do if you wanted to install a phone. Carefully she read the information about how to dial long distance. Dial 1, it said, and the area code . . . Her mind seemed to move very slowly and the booth was stuffy. She felt faint. Then she read another piece of advice: "If you need assistance dial O for Operator." Well, she needed assistance, all right.

She got out the piece of paper with Uncle Arthur's

address on it and read the instructions written on the little circle on the phone. She removed the receiver, inserted a dime, and without much real faith in the results she dialled Operator.

There was a ring and then a voice said, "May I help you?"

She was astonished. The voice sounded as if it were inside her own head.

"Operator," the voice said impatiently. "May I help you?"

"Yes," she said. "Please. I want to talk to Arthur Bent." She read off the address slowly. She waited. There was a long pause and she thought the voice had gone away.

Then it came back again. "Is this a person-to-person call?"

How else would you call someone, if not person to person? "Yes," Laurie said.

"What is your name?"

Why did everybody in the world have to know her name? "Laurie James."

"One moment please." There was a sound of whirring and buzzing. She heard a faint ringing. Again a pause. Then a woman's voice said, "Hello?"

Laurie didn't know whether she was supposed to start talking or not. While she hesitated, the operator said, "I have a call for Mr. Arthur Bent. Is he there?"

"No, he isn't," the woman's voice said.

"When will he be back?"

"He's out of town," the woman said. "He won't be back until Friday."

"Thank you," the operator said. "He's out of town,

ma'am. He won't be back until Friday."

Laurie had lost track of who was talking to whom. She didn't answer.

"Ma'am?" said the operator. "Your party is not in."

"Oh," Laurie said. "Oh. Thank you very much." There was a click. She stood holding the receiver uncertainly. Then she hung it in its cradle. There was a rattle and a clatter as her dime returned. She wondered if it was really hers. Did the telephone company do all that for nothing? She took it anyway and opened the booth door and went out. It was good to get out of there. So Uncle Arthur could not come for her. She wondered vaguely who the woman was that had answered the phone.

Across the street a drugstore was just opening up. A short man was rolling up the corrugated shutters. He opened the door and propped it open. There was something Laurie had intended to buy. She tried to remember what it was. Her head ached badly and it was hard to think. Fly dope, that was it. She went into the store. It was cool inside.

"Good morning," the man said.

"Do you have fly dope?" she asked.

"You bet we do." He went behind the counter and brought out several different kinds of cans.

She picked out the one her grandfather used. "How much is it?"

"Forty-five cents." He put it in a paper sack. "Will there be anything else?"

"No." She counted out the change and gave it to him.

"Looks like you broke your arm," he said.

"No, I just hurt it." She made for the door as fast as she could, feeling that she was going to faint.

She walked unsteadily up the street to Hook. Vince leaned in the doorway of the restaurant watching her. He nodded, but he didn't say anything. She unhitched Hook and tried to get into the saddle but she couldn't make it. She leaned against the horse, her head on his neck, trying to get rid of the dizziness.

"You want I should give you a boot up?" It was Vince.

"Please."

He helped her into the saddle. She looked down at his broad expressionless face. She was grateful for a man who helped without asking questions.

"I thank you very much," she said.

He grinned for the first time. He had one gold tooth in front. Then he stood back and let her ride Hook out onto the street. She looked back and lifted her hand. He just stood there watching her.

She rode to the end of the town and then cut off toward the mountains, hoping she would come to a good camping place soon. She didn't think she could ride very far.

She drooped in the saddle, letting Hook take his own pace. When she came at last to a shady place in the forest, she stopped. Her head ached and she felt groggy and her arm pained some. She took two of the pills the doctor had given her and without bothering to take down her bedroll, lay down on the warm pine needles and went to sleep.

chapter 13

She slept until late afternoon. When she awoke, she felt much better. She sat up and looked around. Hook was standing with his head down, half-dozing. She was in a birch grove, and the light fell through the leaves in dappled patterns.

"I'm hungry," she said to Hook. He jerked his head up as if she had caught him napping.

After building a small fire, she cooked the can of Spam and some of the mashed potatoes. She didn't have a fork for the potatoes, so she made some kind of chopsticks with two twigs. There was no creek, but there was a spring that bubbled up and spread enough water on the ground so that she could clean her frying pan.

She figured by the sun that it must be about five-thirty or six. There was still time to ride for a while. It would not be dark much before ten o'clock, and she had lost so much time.

She sprayed fly dope on herself and on Hook's neck and back, making him sneeze. Then she found a rock to stand on so so she could mount. She rode along feeling better than she had felt for some time. Hook seemed rested, too. He bobbed his head up and down jauntily and stepped out with a smart gait. They made good progress for several hours.

When the sun finally went down, she rode on a little longer in the half-light. She liked that time of day when the trees looked silver, like soft shadows of themselves, and the sky was dark gray. The world seemed softened by some kind of magic touch. She could half hear the night sounds of the animals and she was aware of life all around her.

It would be nice, she thought, to just go on living in the forest forever. And yet there was that other world, the world of people, and although it alarmed her it also was beginning to intrigue her. It was full of things that she would like to know more about. At least, she thought proudly, I have mastered the telephone.

She began to think of what high school would be like. Maybe they wouldn't even let her in since she had never been to regular school. Her grandfather said she might have to take a test, but that was all right; she liked taking tests. And she had gotten good grades on all her correspondence courses except algebra.

But what would it be like to be in school with all those kids? She didn't know how to make friends. Did you just walk up to somebody and say, "I want to be your friend?" It didn't seem likely. Other kids would think she was some kind of maverick probably. She sighed. She knew she was going to have to face it sooner or later. Grandfather was determined that she shouldn't grow up ignorant and she did want to learn. If she had grown up around other children, things might have been different. Sometimes just for a minute she wondered if her grandfather had done the best thing in keeping her in Hawkins Dry Diggings all these years but her loyalty made her reject the notion at once. She certainly would have hated growing up in an orphanage. She had really had a lovely life, free and happy. And most of all she had had her grandfather's loving care. She was a lucky girl.

When she came to a river, she decided she had better camp for the night. Her arm was beginning to ache again. She had to take it out of the sling to get the saddle off. She watered Hook and found him a good place to stay. She ate the last of Miss Emily's good cookies and took two more of Dr. Ashe's pills and lay down under a yellow pine.

In the morning she climbed a hill that was directly in front of her so she could get a good look at what lay ahead. Not very far in the distance she could see the buildings and smokestacks of a city. It must be Missoula. That meant that her journey was more than half over. She got out the map and studied it. She could see no way to go around the city without going way out of her way and maybe getting lost. She would have to go straight through although she didn't like the idea. Still, it was early, not more than five-thirty, she guessed, so perhaps there wouldn't be many people around.

When she rode into town, it was just beginning to stir. To keep on the right route until she got through the city, she had to go right through the center of town. She hoped there was no law about riding horses in town. A few early risers cast curious glances at her, but no one paid much attention. At an intersection a police car pulled up alongside her and she tensed for trouble but the officer gave her a wave and went on.

She paused to look down the main street, astounded. She had no idea that a place could have so many stores. She decided she had to take a look, even if it delayed her a little. She turned Hook to the right and got off and led him so she could look at everything slowly.

Most of the places were closed because of the early hour. She told Hook to stand, and she went to press her nose against the big glass window of a store that sold western gear. She had never seen such magnificent saddles. And boots, all kinds of boots, and western clothes. She looked down at her own worn and dusty jeans and shirt. She had never given any thought to clothes except as something to keep you warm.

She walked slowly down the street. There were men's clothing stores and women's clothing stores and sporting goods stores. One store had a window full of fishing gear, and the wall was covered with tied flies. Grandfather would like to see that.

She passed a very old-looking restaurant that was open. She thought about going in for a cup of coffee but after she took a closer look, she decided against it. It was also a bar and two old men were sitting at the bar talking in loud voices.

She called Hook and kept going down the street. The

stores were getting bigger and bigger and they had all kinds of things in the windows. Furniture, refrigerators and stoves like Miss Emily's, toys that she could never have imagined, just all kinds of stuff. She liked the little toy cars that looked like real pickups and trucks. It seemed remarkable that a person could make them that little and have them look like the real thing, tires and everything.

She passed a place that said "Beauty Salon". She thought a salon was where men went to drink so she was going on by but since it was closed, she decided to look in. It wasn't that kind of place at all, or if it was, it was some new kind that she hadn't heard about. There was a row of open booths on one side with chairs in them that looked a little like the chair in the old abandoned barbershop up at Hawkins Dry Diggings. On the other side of the room were big silver hood-shaped things. She stared at them a long time trying to figure out what in the world they could be.

"I'll have to ask Grandfather," she said to Hook. They crossed an intersection and came to a hotel. The two-story ten-room building at Hawkins was called a hotel, but this thing was enormous. A sign in one of the windows said "Coffee Shop" and she could see lights and people inside. She would surely like a good cup of coffee. Looking around for a place to tie up Hook, she led him around the corner. There were a lot of metal stands in a row at the curb. She read the printing on one of them, which said it was a parking meter. It showed you where to put in a penny or a nickel to park for a certain length of time. The idea of having to pay to park a car astonished her. Didn't everybody own the public streets?

"It doesn't say anything about horses," she said to Hook, "but here goes." She got out a penny and put it in the slot and waited to see what would happen. The little red flag disappeared and a thing like a clock's hand shot up to twenty on the dial. "Now how in tarnation do they do that?" she said. She bent over and tried to see if there was any clue underneath the meter, but it was just solid metal. People certainly figured out the darndest things.

"Well, you're legal for twenty minutes," she said to Hook. She rubbed his nose. He didn't seem too happy to be there. "I won't be long."

She came around to the front of the hotel. A man got out of a car that said TAXI and walked just ahead of her to the door. But it was a very strange door. It had glass compartments and it revolved. The man stepped into one of the compartments so she stepped in right behind him. He looked back at her over his shoulder, surprised. She realized her mistake at once. She should have gone into a separate compartment. She was so ashamed of her ignorance that she forgot to step out of the revolving door when it came around to the inside of the hotel. The man got out and she was left in there, still going around. He looked back and laughed, and then disappeared somewhere inside. She was furious with herself for being so stupid. She stood still for a moment in the door, and then she gave it an angry push. It went so fast she had to almost run, leaping out of it into the hotel just in time. She was out of breath, and she looked around quickly to make sure no one had seen her. There were people in the coffee shop at her right, but they didn't look up.

The hotel was the biggest place she had ever seen. There was a long wide corridor that widened out into a place with lots of big leather chairs and little tables and couches and a big television set that showed color pictures. The carpet under her feet was thick and squishy and red.

A young man in a short white jacket came into the corridor carrying a tray with dishes on it. He looked at her coldly. He pushed a button and a huge door slid open silently, revealing a kind of tiny room. The door closed. Lights went on, over the door, under numbers that went from one to six.

Laurie glanced in a long narrow mirror beside the mysterious door. She was appalled at what she saw. Her hair looked as if she hadn't combed it for a month, her face was streaked with dust, and her clothes looked ready for the rag bag. No wonder the young man had given her a chilly look. Hungry though she was, she could not go into that clean, nice-looking coffee shop. She fled, pushing the revolving door too hard so that she had to make a flying jump for the sidewalk.

When she got around the corner, a man was standing there looking at Hook. The man was wearing faded jeans and old cowboy boots and a battered Stetson. He looked almost as disreputable as Laurie did. When he saw her, he tilted his head toward Hook, and said, "Four cylinders or six?"

She wasn't sure what he meant so she pretended she didn't see him.

He watched her mount up. Then he spat tobacco juice into the dust along the curb and strode off.

She rode back to the intersection and found her southern route. She passed a lot of places that said MOTEL and had little cemented-in pools of water. She wished she could get into some of that water with a bar of soap. She was ashamed to be so dirty.

The road angled off toward the east and then bent south again, where it became a big highway. She had to get off it in a hurry. She wanted to ride along in the pastureland but there was a barbed wire fence. She pulled up two posts, laid the fence flat, and rode Hook across, and then put the posts up again. She hoped no one was going to shoot at her again for trespassing. She had no choice.

The field was dotted with Black Angus grazing quietly. After a while she got further away from the highway into the low foothills. She rode along all day, stopping at noon to rest. She washed in a creek and combed her hair and found some wild blackberries to eat. It was hard going because she did not have as much energy as she used to have. Maybe the long trip was beginning to tell on her.

In the evening she came to a lake and decided to spend the night there. It was a pretty lake, about a mile long, with trees coming down close to the edge. She built her fire down close to the water's edge because the forest was dry and she was being especially careful about fire.

Her pack was getting light. There was nothing left of what Miss Emily had given her except the cocoa and one last lump of sugar, which she gave to Hook. She found some bushes laden with service berries and feasted on those. They were good, but they weren't a meal. She got her gun and walked a little way looking for signs of rabbit but she saw no rabbits. She did come across a ground squirrel—and shot him neatly through the head.

She had never eaten ground squirrel but her grandfather always said that practically any of the animals that roamed the woods of America were good to eat, if you were hungry.

She took him back to the campfire, skinned him out, and cooked the meat. It tasted pretty good.

When she was ready to settle down for the night, she found that she was still very wide awake, so she sat down on a rock near the edge of the lake. There were soft piled-up clouds over her head and their edges were lighted up by the moon hidden behind them. Off beyond the clouds a few stars glittered. Laurie looked at them. When she was a little girl, she used to think that her mother and father had gone away to live on a star and she used to wonder which one it was.

In front of her the dark dreaming water of the lake lay still. Then far out a fish jumped, and the circles started by his leap spread and spread until they ended in a quiet lap of water at her feet.

Somehow she seemed to miss her mother more since she had known Miss Emily. She sat with her chin on her hand staring at the water and trying to remember things about her mother and father, something she had tried many times. It almost seemed that she did remember them, but she knew a lot of it was from looking at their pictures and hearing her grandfather talk about them. Her mother had been, as he often said, "the apple of his eye". He had sent her away to college in Oregon because she wanted to be a teacher, but then she had met and married Dan James. Her grandfather had liked her father. Every summer they came from wherever they had been living and spent part of the vacation with him. "Dan was a great fisherman and a great reader," her grandfather always said. Laurie had been with her grandfather when the accident had happened that killed her parents. She was just barely three. Her grandfather said that she had cried for them for a long time. Many times she still felt like crying for them.

She got up. There was no sense sitting there feeling sorry for herself. She threw her blanket down onto the ground and lay down, but still she could not sleep. She wished she had Miss Emily to share such a beautiful spot with her. She wondered if Miss Emily ever camped out.

She thought about Kicking Horse and hoped he had had enough supper. It would be nice to have him with her, too. When she had been alone all the time, as she had been most of her life, she had taken it for granted and hardly minded it. But now the more she saw of people, the more lonely she felt when she was by herself. She fell asleep pondering this paradox.

chapter 14

The sun blazing hotly in her eyes woke her. It looked like an orange Necco wafer in the sky. She put up her arm to shield her eyes. A hot wind had come up. Since she had slept later than usual, she considered skipping breakfast, but she was hungry. She dug a fishhook out of her pack and found a dead branch of a tree that would serve as a pole when she stripped off the twigs. She dug until she found a fat worm, then took off her jeans and waded into the lake with her homemade pole. She knew there were plenty of fish; she had heard them jumping in the night.

She fished for about ten minutes without any luck. The lake was shallow so she waded out farther, deciding to give herself five more minutes. If nothing bit, she would forget it. It wouldn't kill her to miss a meal. She waded over to a little cove. She cast and waited, pulling the line up very slowly.

Then she felt the pull. She played the fish in with great care. At last she had him. It was a lake bass, not a very big one, but it would do for breakfast. She took it ashore and killed it with a sharp blow with a rock as her grandfather had taught her to do. After cleaning the fish, she built a small fire on the sand. The fish was good. While she had the fire going, she boiled some water for her canteen and then shook it up to get some of the oxygen back into it so it wouldn't taste flat. She stamped out the fire and poured panful after panful of water on it until it was completely dead.

"There," she said to Hook. "We're ready for another day."

She consulted her compass and map. If she followed the line of the lake to just beyond the cove where she had caught the fish and then struck off into the woods she would be on the right track. She mounted Hook and took a last look around to make sure she had not forgotten anything. Hook started to go.

"Wait," she said. She reined him in. She was looking at a small white plume of smoke that was rising into the sky back in the direction from which she had come. It was not very far away. Frowning she watched it. And as she watched the white smoke changed to billowing clouds of dark yellow. She listened intently. Then she heard the terrifying crack and roar of a forest fire.

The wind was toward the lake. She had seen forest fires many times, and she knew with what frightening speed they spread. Though this was small, it could soon be upon her. She could see from the smoke that it was moving south and west and already she could feel the heat and hear the crashing of trees. She didn't know where to go. Fires were tricky things; they could change direction in an instant. She saw a pine tree ignite and go up like a blazing torch. Flaming pieces of bark flew through the air.

"We've got to get out of here," she said. She rode Hook into the lake. Perhaps it would not be a big fire, and they could sit it out in the water until they saw what direction it was taking. Hook didn't like it. He reared and when he came down, his front feet sent up a great spray of water.

"Cut that out," Laurie said. "Just settle down now." She rode him out into the lake until the water was up around his withers, wrapping her feet around the saddle horn to keep dry and turning Hook so she could watch the progress of the fire.

The flames swept down to the east shore of the lake. Pine trees were igniting in great explosions of flame. Trees fell across each other in a tangle of blackened branches. The air was dense with thick smoke and the lake was deluged with flying sparks and ash and debris. It was stiflingly hot. She moved Hook a little farther out but it began to get deep and she didn't dare go any farther. The smoke made her cough, and the heat made the air shimmer. She leaned over, dipped her sling into the water and wiped her face with it, breathing into its coolness for a moment. She wet it again and mopped Hook's head and neck. He was standing still now, but he quivered all over. A live spark fell on his neck and he started violently. Laurie put the wet cloth on it.

It seemed like a long time that she stayed there in the lake watching the devastation. She thought about the wayfaring stranger and wondered if he had been caught in the fire. Somehow she expected to see him riding out of the flames singing, "This is my story, this is my song." Maybe he had even been responsible for starting it. A lot of forest fires came from human carelessness.

The fire seemed to be spreading toward the north now, burning along the shore to her left. She wondered if she dared go ashore to the south and try to get away. She decided she had better wait. The wind could change again and she would be trapped.

Then she heard a plane. When she first saw it, it was quite high, but it began a sharp descent, coming in from the north. It dove into a cloud of smoke and then in a few minutes it lifted above the smoke again. She saw a man jump from the plane. She held her breath. He seemed to plummet straight down toward the fire, but then his parachute opened, bobbing in the sky like a great white umbrella. He floated down with leisurely ease. In a minute he was followed by another man, and then another. The plane circled and disappeared, the thrum of its engine still audible.

The men were smoke jumpers. She knew about smoke jumpers. She had seen their planes near Hawkins Dry Diggings, and her grandfather had told her about them. They trained in a forest service program at Missoula and then went out to put out forest fires, not only in Montana but all over the northwest. She had never seen them so close before, though, and she wondered what they did after they hit the ground. She wished she could watch them but once they got into the trees there were no signs of them. However, in a few minutes the appearance of the smoke began to change. It became dense and black and then it began to subside. Whatever they were doing seemed to work. When her grandfather was a young man, he had been a fire lookout for a while, living all alone on top of a mountain in a kind of tree house. His place had been struck by lightning so often he said he didn't even look up unless he smelled something burning.

When the fire seemed to be under control, she turned Hook toward the south shore of the lake.

"We'd better get out of here," she told him. "They might think it was our fault that the fire got started."

Hook was glad to get out of the cold water. She followed the shore of the lake for a way, along an area that had not burned, just in case the fire started up again, but when it finally seemed to be safe she cut south.

That night she found a rabbit for her dinner, but she was even more careful than usual about fire. She built it so close to the creek where she had stopped that the dampness of the sand kept putting the fire out. She finally got a small one going and cooked her rabbit. If she were at home her grandfather would have cooked his famous hassenpfeffer. But never mind—the roasted rabbit was good.

Since she was covered with soot from the fire, she bathed in the creek and washed her hair as well as she could. In the creek, a shallow stream with tawny rocks strewn all over it, she stepped from rock to rock until she was in the deepest part of the water. Hook splashed around in the shallows, sidestepping and backing up when she came to catch him, splashing water on her.

"For a horse," she said, "you've got a good sense of humor." He put his nose in her hand. "Nope, the sugar is all gone. You'll have to wait till we get to Uncle Arthur's. If we ever do."

She was tired. If she had known how long it was going to take, she was not sure she would have had the courage to start out. And yet something had to be done. There was that doctor in Libby who had treated her for the whooping cough and the other time when she got the flu. Perhaps she should have gone to him. But he probably would have sent Grandfather to a hospital, and then somebody would have decided they had to do something about her, and there would have been all that mess. She guessed her grandfather was right about sending her to Uncle Arthur. But it was a long way.

chapter 15

In the middle of the next day Laurie came to a camp-ground. There were picnic tables and fieldstone fireplaces and piped-in water and rest rooms. People sure went to a lot of trouble to make things fancy. If they wanted to camp out, why didn't they just camp out? Still it was nice. She took a long drink of the good cold water and filled her canteen. She built a fire in one of the fireplaces and made some cocoa. Then she took a little time to explore.

Off in the woods at the end of a grass-covered road there was a small trailer. No one seemed to be around, but she kept an eye on it.

She rested for a while, lying on the warm pine needles.

It was a nice place. Before she left she put her face under the cold water and let the water run for a minute.

"There," she said to Hook, as she came up dripping, "I guess I'm ready to go." She hated to leave the quiet sheltering place, but she got into the saddle and rode down the grassy lane until she heard a car coming. She veered off into the trees and waited while the car went by, a yellow pickup with the Montana Forest Service emblem on the door.

A little farther along the road, in a place where a tiny waterfall trickling down a slope had made the ground muddy, she saw prints. She stopped Hook and studied them. She wasn't absolutely sure but they looked to her like mule prints.

"And," she said aloud to Hook, "not too many people go riding around the country on mules." She left the road and after a few minutes she came to a game trail that ran more or less parallel to the road. She could hear a river off to her right, and she rode over to take a look at it. It was a wide foaming river down in a deep canyon. The cliff on which she stood dropped away sharply to the bottom. On the other side of the river a mountain reared abruptly upward so that the river was in shadow.

She went back to the game trail and continued on, keeping her senses alert for sight or sound of the man on the mule.

A magpie swooped in front of her, flashing his shining black and white plumage. Hook shied. "Steady, boy," she said, "it's only an old magpie."

The limbs of the trees hung low and she had to ride slowly, parting them so she could get through. All at once she thought she heard something. She stopped and listened. It sounded like a child crying. Then someone called "Mama!" It came from the direction of the river. She looped Hook's reins around a tree and went on foot to see what it was, moving carefully, not knowing what she might meet. But she saw no one. She went to the edge of the cliff and looked down. A few feet below her on a narrow ledge huddled a small child. Her face was tear-stained, and when she saw Laurie, she began to howl.

"How did you get down there?" Laurie said.

The little girl stopped crying. "I fell down."

"Where are your parents?" She was testing the edge of the cliff cautiously with her foot.

"They're lost," the little girl said. She wailed again.

"Stop crying," Laurie said sharply. She was afraid the child would fall off the ledge. There was a long drop to the foaming river. Laurie lay down on her stomach and reached her hand down. She could just barely touch the child. She didn't dare move out any further on the ledge or she would fall over herself. But there had to be a way. She thought of the rope she always carried.

"Don't move and don't cry," she said sternly to the little girl. "I'm going to get you out of there. Just stay still a minute."

"Are you going to get my mama?" the little girl asked.

"We'll find her as soon as I get you out of there."

Laurie ran back to Hook and unsnapped the strap that held the lariat.

"Why does everything happen to me," she said.

She ran back and tied one end of the rope around a sturdy pine, talking to the the little girl all the time that she was doing it. She measured the distance, and then tied the other end of the rope around her own waist.

Now if she slipped over the edge, she could make it back up with the rope. But she had better not slip; if she did, the child might fall.

Very slowly and cautiously, talking steadily to reassure herself as much as the little girl, she inched out over the edge. "Hold your arms up straight," she said. The little girl held up her arms. "Now when I get hold of you, I want you to grab my arms. Don't grab me around the neck. Take hold of my arms tight and hold on. Understand? And don't grab this arm too high up." She moved her injured arm.

"Understand," the little girl said. She was watching Laurie with bright intelligent eyes.

Laurie lay out over the ledge as far as she dared. She tried not to look at the dizzy drop below her as she reached down first one arm and then the other. "Try not to grab me where the bandage is," she said, warning the child again.

"Did you fall down and hurt yourself?" the child said.

"Yes." She touched the child's hands. First the little girl took hold of her wrists. She felt the tight grip of the small hands. "That's right. Now move your hands up my arms, up above the elbows. That's the way. You're doing fine." When the child had a good hold, Laurie began to pull up. It was a terrible strain on her shoulders and back, and her wounded arm hurt. She was not sure she could do it. Then she got her good arm around the child's waist and that gave her more leverage. She began inching backward on the edge of the cliff.

The little girl said, "Ouch!" as her knees scraped the rocks of the cliff.

"Hang on," Laurie said. "We'll have you up in a minute." She used her free hand to hold onto the rope, pulling herself up with it. The child was small, but she was dead weight. When Laurie had moved back far enough so that she was not in danger of falling, she put her other hand under the child's arm and put all her strength into a great heave upward. The child cleared the top of the cliff. Laurie fell over backward, the little girl on top of her. Laurie lay still a minute, trying to get her breath.

The little girl sat up. "Well," she said calmly, "we did it."

Laurie laughed with relief. "We sure did." Her voice trembled from the exertion, and her arm was throbbing. "Now what am I going to do with you?" She sat up and untied the rope.

"Take me home. I want Mama."

"Where do you live?"

"I live in Montana," the child said, proud of her knowledge.

"Holy Pete!" Laurie said. "Montana is a big place." She took the child's hand and led her toward Hook. "How old are you?"

The little girl held up three fingers. "I'm this many."

"What's your name?"

"Sandy."

"Sandy what?"

She thought a minute. "Patterson. I have a Mama and a Daddy and a dog named Harry. Harry is my best friend in all the world."

Laurie was trying to think what to do with her. The road that led from the campground probably went to a town. She guessed she would just have to take her into town and see if she could find her parents. She prayed that they would not run across the stranger.

"Is that your horse?" Sandy asked.

"Yes."

"Do I get to ride it? Sometimes my daddy lets me ride on his horse with him." She looked up at Laurie, excited. She had short red-blonde hair and green eyes. She was a very pretty little girl. Her parents should take better care of her, Laurie thought.

"How did you get way out here anyway?" Laurie swung Sandy up onto the front of the saddle.

"We went on a picnic. I went to look for flowers. I found some pretty flowers, but I dropped them down that big hole when I fell down. Can we go get my flowers?"

"Not now," Laurie said. "We have to find your mama." She swung into the saddle. She had not wanted to go into town. It meant another delay. And who knew what all this with the little girl would lead to. But she had no choice. She wished the Forest Service truck would come back; then she could turn the child over to them.

Sandy looked around at her. "You are my very best friend," she said.

Laurie couldn't help smiling. "I thought Harry was your very best friend."

"And you, too," Sandy said. She leaned back comfortably against Laurie. "What is your horsie's name?"

"Hook."

"Fishhook?"

"Just plain Hook."

Hook flicked his ears at hearing his name. Laurie got

away from the game trail and went back to the road.

"I'm hungry," Sandy said.

"So am I, as a matter of fact," Laurie said.

"I'm thirsty, too," Sandy said.

Laurie unscrewed the top of the canteen and gave her a drink. The water ran down her chin and made rivulets in the dirt on her face.

"That was good," she gasped. "Do you have any purple juice?"

"No, I don't."

"Purple juice is my favorite," Sandy said.

They came at last to the main road where there were some road signs. The nearest town was four miles north. That meant she would have to back-track. Eight extra miles altogether. She groaned wearily. But then she noticed another sign that said, "Butte— 20 miles". Maybe she would get there after all. Twenty miles was not so bad. If only she could strike right out for Butte and not do all this back-tracking. A car whizzed past them. For a moment she thought of hailing a car and asking them to take Sandy home. But she dismissed the idea. Who knew what kind of people they might be. They might hurt the child or kidnap her or something.

The child lay limp against her, and Laurie saw that she had fallen asleep. Poor little kid, she thought; she must have been awfully scared. She was a game little girl. Laurie liked her. She turned Hook north.

chapter 16

The town looked much like the others. Stores and gas stations were strung out along a main street, and radiating from it were the streets where people lived. It struck Laurie that people didn't have much imagination when they laid out their towns. Now if I were going to make a town, she thought, I'd think of something new. Like make a store look like the Taj Mahal or something like that. And have more trees and grass around.

"Sandy," she said. "Wake up, Sandy."

"Mama," Sandy said sleepily.

"No, I'm Laurie. Wake up and tell me where you live."

Sandy sat up abruptly, blinking. She looked all around as if she could not remember how she got where she was.

She gave Laurie a long stare.

"Is this the town where you live?" Laurie hoped that it wouldn't turn out to be the wrong town.

Sandy looked around. "There's Mr. Jennings' pickup," she said. "He's got rabbits."

Then it was the right town. "Now show me where you live."

"This is downtown," Sandy said.

"Where is your house?"

"Down that street."

Laurie turned down the street Sandy pointed to. It was a tree-lined residential street with small well-kept houses.

"Which house?"

Sandy looked up and down. "I don't think it's this street."

"Are you sure it isn't?"

"Our house isn't here."

Laurie rode back to the center of town and continued north. A ways up they came to the police station. She could take Sandy there of course, but there would be all those questions. She was too close to Butte to risk being stopped.

Sandy pointed. "There's my daddy's car. I want to see my daddy." There was a blue station wagon parked in front of the police station.

There was no way out of it. Laurie turned in to the police station. What if she just put Sandy in the car and rode away? Her father would find her. But Sandy might be wrong about the car as she had been about the street.

Laurie dismounted and lifted Sandy down. Things certainly got complicated when you got out among people.

Sandy danced over to the car and jiggled the door handle. "Where's my daddy?" she said.

"Maybe he's inside," Laurie said. She took Sandy by the hand and led her up the broken steps of the police station. It was a dilapidated, dirty, whitewashed building. Inside there were two offices and in the hall a big bulletin board with posters of wanted men on it. Laurie wanted to stop and look at the pictures, but she kept going. One room said "Radio Room." She didn't want to listen to any radio, so she chose the other door. A burly policeman was talking to an old man.

"We'll look into it, Mr. Summers," he was saying.

The old man talked and talked, almost unintelligibly. Laurie was too nervous to listen to him. The officer kept saying, "Sure, Mr. Summers, we'll look into it. We sure will."

Finally the old man shuffled out still mumbling. The policeman mopped his face with a handkerchief. He looked at Laurie. "Yes?"

"I found this little girl in the woods," Laurie said. "I wonder if . . . "

The officer looked down at Sandy, and his indifference disappeared.

"Say," he said, "aren't you Sandy Patterson?"

"Yes," Sandy said. "And I'm this many." She held up three fingers.

"Come in the other room," he said to Laurie. He strode ahead of her into the Radio Room. What now, Laurie thought. For a wild second she thought of leaving Sandy there and making a run for it. But they would catch her. She would be a fugitive from justice.

Another policeman was behind the high counter in the

Radio Room. He was older, bald, and tired-looking.

"It's the Patterson kid," the first officer said. "This kid found her."

Both policemen looked intently first at Sandy and then at Laurie.

"That's my daddy's car," Sandy said. "I want my daddy."

"You better call the searchers back," the first policeman said. "Get those Forest Service guys back. Where's her folks at now?"

"They just went home. Appleton took them home," the older man said. "Mr. Patterson was out hunting for her all night. He's about played out."

"Better call them."

The older policeman picked up a microphone and began to talk. Laurie wanted to hear what he said, but the other man was on the phone.

"Get me the Pattersons," he said. "We've found the kid."

"I'm thirsty," Sandy said. She tugged at Laurie's hand. In the hall beyond the door there was a drinking fountain. She pulled Laurie toward it.

The younger policeman put his hand over the phone's mouthpiece. "Hey, where are you going?" he said.

"She's thirsty," Laurie said.

When she brought Sandy back, the policeman had finished talking on the phone.

"You kids sit here," he said, indicating a bench. "Your daddy will be here in a minute, honey."

"Can't I go?" Laurie said.

"Pretty soon, pretty soon." He got out a big block of paper. "Now where did you find the little girl?"

Laurie described the place as well as she could. She explained that Sandy had fallen over the cliff.

"That's why nobody saw her," the policeman said. "O.K. How did you get her out?"

"She pulled me with a rope," Sandy said. "It was scary, but I didn't cry, did I, Laurie?"

"No. You were brave."

"I was brave," Sandy said to the policeman.

A thin young man with a big camera slung over his shoulder burst into the room.

"Hey," he said, "I hear you found the Patterson kid." He looked at Sandy. "Are you Sandy Patterson?"

"Yes," Sandy said. "This is Laurie; she is my very best friend."

"Look this way a second, both of you," the man said. There was a flash of light. Laurie jumped. "It's all right," the man said. "I got a picture."

"What for?" Laurie said. The flash had given her a fright.

"For the newspaper, honey. You'll be in the paper."

"I don't want to be in the paper," Laurie said.

"It's the price of fame, honey." He winked at the policeman.

"Hold off a minute, Terry, and let me get this fact sheet finished," the policeman said. "What's your name?" He was looking over his glasses at Laurie.

Here we go, she thought. "Laurie James." She didn't dare make up a name for the police. For all she knew, it might be a crime.

"Address?"

She hesitated, and he said impatiently, "Where do you live?"

"Hawkins Dry Diggings, Montana."

The newspaper man said, "You're putting us on. There can't be any such place."

That made Laurie angry. "He asked me where I came from," she said coldly, "and I told him."

"But where is it at?" the newspaperman said.

"Up north."

"You got any more questions, Jake?" the newspaperman said.

Jake seemed to have lost interest. "No," he said.

"I got a few more," said the newspaperman.

Laurie looked at the policeman. "Do I have to answer them?"

He shrugged. "Not if you don't want to."

"Oh, come on, honey," the man said. "You're a heroine. Let's have the story."

"There isn't any more," Laurie said.

"Look," the man said.

The policeman interrupted. "If she don't want to, she don't want to."

"Can I go now?" Laurie said to the policeman.

Before he could answer, a man and a woman swept into the room. The woman scooped Sandy up in her arms and began to cry. "Baby, baby," she said.

The man put out his hand and touched Sandy's cheek. "Hi, sweetheart."

"Mama!" Sandy cried. "Daddy!" She struggled to be put down, and her mother let her slide to the floor.

Again there was the brilliant flash of the newspaperman's light bulb.

Laurie sidled toward the door. Perhaps in the confusion she could get away unnoticed. But Sandy's father put out his hand and stopped her.

"Is this the girl that found Sandy?"

"That's Laurie," Sandy said. "I love her. She's got a horse named Hook, and I like him next to Harry. Daddy, can I have a horse?"

Her father laughed. "At this moment, baby, you name it and you can have it." He seized Laurie's hand and shook it. "How can we ever thank you?"

"It wasn't anything." Laurie tried to pull away, but he held her hand tightly.

"To us it was everything," Sandy's mother said. Her voice was still shaky and she clung to Sandy's hand.

"I almost fell in the river," Sandy said proudly.

"I hope you've learned a lesson, young lady," her father said, trying to sound stern. "No more wandering off."

"George," Sandy's mother said, "give Laurie something."

"Sure," he said heartily. "You bet I will." He reached in his pocket and pulled out a wad of bills.

Laurie was shocked. She backed away.

"I don't want anything," she said, "not for a thing like that."

"Listen," he said, "you saved our child's life. She's our only child. You don't know what you did for us. Nothing we could do would be enough . . ." He choked up. He thrust some money into Laurie's hand.

"Please," she said, "I don't want it."

There was confusion in the hall, the sound of voices and the scuffling of feet. Then an officer came in, leading a man by the arm. Laurie looked up at them and her heart almost stopped. It was the wayfaring stranger. His glance met hers for a moment and then swept on to the officer behind the desk.

"What have you got there?" the man behind the desk said.

"A case of vagrancy," the officer said.

"He's got me wrong," the stranger said, in his loud strident voice. "I am a man of God."

Sandy's mother touched Laurie's arm. "Can we take you anywhere or do anything for you?"

"No, thanks," Laurie said. "I've got my horse." She was watching the stranger out of the corner of her eye.

"We'll say good-bye then," Sandy's mother said. "And if you ever come through town again or if there is ever anything we can do for you, please let us know."

Laurie gave her a quick smile. The woman was nice, but Laurie had her mind on the stranger.

"Then I'll take this baby on home and put her to bed," Sandy's mother was saying. "She must be exhausted." She held out her hand to Laurie. "Thank you again."

Sandy threw Laurie a kiss. "Come and play with me soon," she said. "You're my very best friend." She and her mother went on out.

"I'll be right along," Sandy's father said to them. He was listening to the stranger.

"Does the man need a lawyer?" he said to the policeman.

"Do you want a lawyer?" the policeman asked the stranger.

"I got no money for lawyers," the stranger said. "I stand here innocent as the newborn babe. I got my God to look after me." He swept around and pointed his long bony finger at Laurie. "This little lady knows me. She can tell you I am a true messenger of the Lord."

Sandy's father, who had started out the door, stopped and looked back. "Do you know this man?" he said to Laurie.

"I have seen him," Laurie said.

"That's good enough for me," the man said. "If Laurie vouches for this man, I'll pay his fine, whatever it is, Al. Just let me know."

"I don't vouch for him," Laurie said. But her words were lost in the hubbub. The stranger lifted his voice.

"The good Lord has come to my rescue again," he said. He wrung the hand of Sandy's father, who looked as if he would like to get out of there. "The Lord will provide. I thank you, sir, you are obviously a good Christian and a servant of the Lord."

Sandy's father pulled his hand loose.

"Let us know if there's anything I can do for you, Laurie," he said. And then he was gone.

"Am I free to go on my way?" the stranger said.

"Where you going?" the policeman said.

"Butte. The place I call home."

The policeman looked down for a moment. Then he said, "All right, get out of here."

"Hallelujah!" shouted the stranger. "Righteousness will triumph."

"You'd better get going," the policeman said, "before I change my mind."

The stranger headed for the door. He paused for a second and looked at Laurie. He raised his battered black hat in an elaborate salute, his eyes glittering. Then he swept on out the door. As he went away, his voice came back to them: "This is my story, this is my song . . ."

The policeman shook his head. "A real kook," he said. He looked at Laurie. "How come you to know him?"

"I don't really know him," she said. "I just bumped into him a couple of times." She wondered if she ought to tell the policeman how the stranger had tried to steal her gold nuggets. She decided to let well enough alone.

"I suppose he's harmless," the policeman said, "but if I was you, I'd keep out of his way."

"Yes," Laurie said, "I plan to." She looked down at the money in her hand. "They ought not to have given me money," she said. "You don't want to get paid for a thing like that."

He shrugged. "He can afford it. He's a lawyer with a pretty good practice. It's their only kid."

"But you don't save somebody's life for money."

"Don't knock it, kid," he said. "Money you can always use."

She walked slowly to the door. As she was going out, he said, "Good luck."

chapter 17

When she was outside, Laurie looked at the money that was crumpled up in her hand—three ten-dollar bills. Thirty dollars. She had never imagined having so much money. It still didn't seem right to her, but the policeman ought to know. She folded it small and put it in her shirt pocket.

She got Hook and rode him slowly back down the main street. Well, she had met the police and escaped without trouble. By the time the newspaper came out, she would be with Uncle Arthur, so anybody who got, as her grandfather would say, "nosey", could be taken care of. But there was the wayfaring stranger somewhere up ahead of her.

Since she had been responsible for getting him out of a fix, maybe he would leave her alone. But she rode slowly just the same, not anxious to overtake him. She began to think about her grandfather. She hoped he was getting along all right. It worried her to have him there alone. She hoped he had enough to eat and that he would not fall or anything, and that Uncle Arthur would go get him right away. Above all she hoped Uncle Arthur would be at home when she got there. She was not sure exactly what he did now. For a while he was a traveling salesman for a hardware company; then he owned a filling station; then he ran a riding school. He seemed to do well at all of them. Her grandfather said, "Arthur is a rolling stone, but he always lands right side up." He always had a new car and he sent money to her grandfather quite often. She had not seen him for about a year. She liked him and would be glad to see him. But most of all she wanted him to be there.

At the south end of town she saw a small café. A truck was parked in front of it. She could smell food cooking and decided to go in.

"Boy," she said to Hook, as she hitched him, "I am really getting brave."

She went inside. Two truck drivers sat at one end of the counter laughing and talking with the waitress, a middle-aged woman with strawlike hair and the thinnest eyebrows Laurie had ever seen.

Laurie slid onto a stool at the other end of the counter. She was so hungry she could hardly stand it. There was a menu lying on the counter, and she picked it up and read it all through. There sure were a lot of things to choose from. She couldn't decide what to have. Everything seemed to cost a lot of money, but she did have thirty dollars.

After a long time the waitress came and stood in front of her. She didn't look at Laurie. She kept glancing back at the truck drivers and smirking. The men were not paying much attention to her.

"What's yours?" she said abruptly.

"I would like to have this steak," Laurie said. "This one here." She pointed to the menu.

"How you want it?" the woman said.

Laurie was puzzled. Should she say "very much"? She hesitated, trying to think what the woman meant.

The woman looked at her impatiently. "Rare, medium, well?"

"Medium," Laurie said. It seemed like a safe answer. She couldn't say "I like it the way Grandpa cooks it."

"Fries or mashed?"

"Fries," Laurie said. Her grandfather fried potatoes in little paper-thin wedges till they were golden brown.

"What kind of dressing?"

Again Laurie was confused. Dressing for what? "What kinds have you got?" she said. That might give her a clue.

"French, Russian, roquefort."

"Russian," Laurie said. Salad dressing, that was what she meant.

"Drink?"

"Milk, please." She was glad she could give at least one right prompt answer. The woman wrote it down and thrust the slip onto a spindle in the little opening that led to the kitchen. "Steak medium," she yelled loudly, although the cook was only a few feet away from her. She went back to her truck drivers.

Laurie picked up the menu and read it all through again. It all sounded good. When she had finished reading the menu, she read the labels on all the little cereal boxes that stood in a row on a shelf behind the counter. There were sure a lot of them. Her grandfather always brought home either corn flakes or shredded wheat. She studied the row of big chrome handles. One said COCA COLA, one said PEPSI, and one said ROOT BEER. She watched the waitress refill the truck drivers' coffee cups.

One of the men came over and stood behind Laurie playing the pinball machine. She turned to watch him, wondering what the point of the game was. He looked up and grinned at her—a big square-shouldered man with grease on his hands.

"I never got no luck," he said.

She smiled politely and turned away. She didn't feel up to any kind of conversation with anybody.

Laurie thought she would faint with hunger if that woman didn't bring her food pretty soon. Finally the woman picked up a plate and shoved it in front of Laurie. She held a glass under another unmarked chrome handle and milk foamed into the glass.

Laurie tried not to gobble; her grandfather had said it was bad manners to gobble. But she could hardly restrain herself from shoveling the food into her mouth. The fries were not like Grandfather's, but she ate them hungrily anyway. The salad was good. But the best thing was the juicy steak. She could feel herself gaining energy with every bite. "A steak will make a new woman of you," her grandfather always said. And she believed it. She drank all of the cold milk and ate every crumb of the bread and butter.

"Look at that kid tuck it away," said the man who had been playing the pinball machine. "She'd make a good truck driver." The other man laughed but the waitress didn't smile.

When Laurie was through, she stood up. The woman came and looked at her expectantly. "How much is it?" Laurie said.

"It's right on the check." The woman pushed a piece of paper toward Laurie.

Laurie looked at it. She hadn't known about checks. It seemed like a waste of paper when the woman could just as well have told her. Scrawled in pencil was "Steak med" and the price, $1.45. Laurie pulled her bills from her shirt pocket. She had to take them all out because they were folded inside each other. The waitress watched her closely as Laurie put a ten dollar bill on the counter. The woman rang it up on the cash register and counted out the change. Laurie put the money back in her pocket.

As she went out the door, she heard the woman say loudly, "Where do kids get all their money nowadays? They carry it around like it's bubble gum."

One of the men said, "Maybe the kid's a gambler. Plays the ponies." He laughed at his own joke.

Laurie went down the steps.

"Why did she have to be so mean?" she said to Hook. "I never did anything to her." She touched him with her heels, and they rode out of town at a fast trot.

chapter 18

Laurie rode along the grassy area that bordered the road. But many cars were whizzing along, and Hook was very nervous. She headed into grassland again. She wished there were woods but the land had become flatter and much more open. At least if the stranger lay in wait for her anywhere, she'd be able to see him.

She got to a clump of pine trees and stopped to think. She almost wished she had told the policeman about the man, about how he tried to get her gold nuggets, but the man would have denied it probably and a policeman would believe an adult before he'd believe her. Still, she wished she had told him. She knew she could outrun the stranger—Hook could leave any old mule standing still in his tracks. But he might catch her unawares.

She decided to hide the gold. Where though? She thought of and discarded several possibilities. Then she thought of her sling. She had not worn it for a while, but she decided to put it back on. She got it out of the pack. It was wrinkled and dirty, but it would do. She took off the chain and the pouch with the gold nuggets and tucked it into the corner of the sling where her elbow fitted. The sling was bulky enough so that the bulge didn't show. She put her one remaining silver dollar in the heel of one boot and in the other boot she put the bills that were left from those Mr. Patterson had given her. She left the change in her wallet.

It was bothersome having the sling on again. But it might turn out to be worth it.

Because she had eaten so much at the café she decided she did not need to worry about lunch. She hoped that if she kept going she might get to Butte by dark. She stopped frequently to check on her direction. Since she was so close, she didn't want to take any chances on getting lost. If she listened intently, she could usually hear the traffic of the highway.

The day grew warm and humid. Thunderclouds piled up in the west. When she came to a drainage ditch, she stopped to let Hook drink, relaxing in the saddle while he bent his long neck to the water. She was very tired. She hoped she could get to Butte that night. One more day seemed more than she could stand.

They crossed an open field where Hereford cattle grazed. One curious calf loped over toward them and then took fright and ran away again, stumbling and bawling as if the devil were after him.

She thought about taking the sling off. Her earlier worry seemed silly suddenly. But it was more trouble to take it off than to leave it on so she didn't bother. She was drooping in the saddle, sometimes almost lulled to sleep by the motion. Once she caught herself starting to slide off. She sat up straight and forced her eyes open.

She tried to think about happy things that would keep her awake. She remembered the time when she was about ten and she and her grandfather had gone fishing and she caught more fish than he did; he had made a crown of daisies for her and proclaimed her the Queen of the Fish.

She remembered the time he took her to the circus. He didn't usually risk taking her to towns, but he said every kid should see a circus. She had liked the trapeze artists best. And the parade with all the animals. Her grand-father had gotten into conversation with one of the circus men, and the man had lifted her up to sit for a moment on the back of the giraffe. It was like sitting on top of a great tower. She had had such a wonderful day that she had been carsick on the way home.

Then at the other end of things there had been the snowy night when she discovered Keats. Going through her father's books, she had found a slender leather-covered volume that she had not noticed before. She sat up late in front of the hot stove reading "La Belle Dame Sans Merci" and "Hyperion" and the sonnets, too excited to go to bed. Once her grandfather called out to her that it was late, but she had read on.

She came to a grove of cottonwood trees. They were the biggest cottonwoods she had ever seen. She decided to stop for a minute and stretch her legs. She dismounted and led Hook through the grove. It was cooler there.

Suddenly Hook jerked back on the reins. She turned to see what was wrong. Before she could move, the wayfaring stranger leaped out from behind a tree with a triumphant yell and grabbed her. She struggled but his long wiry arms were like steel. Hook whinnied and danced backward.

The man had her free arm pinioned behind her back. His dark face was close to hers. He had a metallic smell. Twisting her head away she tried again to get free. She kicked at him, but he was too close for the kicks to be effective.

"All right, little lady," he said. He was breathing hard. "I'll just take that gold."

"That's stealing," she said.

"I take it for God's work," he said. "All the goods of the earth—yea, the minerals in the earth—belong to Him. Where is it?" He reached for the chain that she had worn around her neck and found it gone. He was angry. "What have you done with it?"

"I lost it," she said. She hoped it was not wicked to lie when you were in a tight spot.

"Lost it!" He shook her furiously. "You're lying."

"No, it's gone. I lost it on the trail. A couple of days ago."

He went through her pockets with one hand, holding her tight with the other. He pulled out her wallet and shook it open and the change flew out on the ground. He threw the wallet on the ground.

"It's somewhere," he said. "You've hidden it." Still holding her, he pulled her toward Hook and got the rope. He tied her up and sat her down with her back to a tree. Then he started going through her pack. He threw everything on the ground after he had examined it. Miss Emily's sweater fell in a heap near Laurie's feet. He pulled the bedroll apart. He picked up the pack and went through it again, working fast, his big long-fingered hands tearing at things. His face worked, and he was sweating. He ran his hands over the saddle and Hook backed away.

Finally he turned toward Laurie, his face dark with fury and frustration. His hat had fallen off and his tangled hair was wild. His eyes glittered.

"Where is it?"

She was very frightened. She thought he might kill her. "I told you, I lost it. The chain must have broken."

He glared at her as if he might spring on her and tear her to pieces. "Where did you get it? Is there more where that came from?"

"No," she said. "My grandfather dug it up years ago. He hasn't got any more."

"I could hold you for ransom," he said. "He'd have to give me some gold to get you back."

She struggled to keep her voice calm. "It wouldn't do you any good. He doesn't have anything."

"I need that gold!" His voice was almost a scream.

"It's gone," she said.

He kicked her foot, a hard kick that hurt. "Then sit here and rot," he said. He strode off into the trees, and in a few minutes she saw him riding away on the mule.

She leaned her head back against the rough tree trunk. She was trembling all over, and soon she began to cry, tears of relief and of reaction to the fear she had felt.

After a few minutes she straightened up. She had to get out of there somehow, or as he had said, she might rot. Examining the rope, she found that in his haste he had not done a very effective job. If she could just get hold of the end, which was just barely out of her reach, she thought she could get loose. She worked her shoulders back and forth, trying to loosen the rope. At first nothing seemed to happen. Then she felt a slight loosening. She kept it up. It hurt her arm; he had wound the rope right over her wound; but she kept up her rocking motion. Then she tried again to reach the end of the rope. This time her fingers touched it.

She wriggled sideways and then back and forth, and reached for the rope end again. Getting hold of it, she pulled at it and it began to come loose. For about ten minutes she worked. It was a strain on her patience. Several times it seemed as if she was not going to be able to get free, but finally she got it loose enough so that she could wriggle her way out of it. She stood up, stretching her cramped muscles. She was free!

She called Hook, gathered up her things, and walked with him a little way through the cottonwood grove. It was too late to make it to Butte before dark, that was certain. And she was not anxious to overtake her captor on the way. The country was mostly open, without the protection of forest. So she decided to spend the night among the trees she had found and get into Butte in the morning.

"Well," she said to Hook, "that was an experience." She took her arm out of the sling and left the sling hanging around her neck, the pouch with the gold nuggets securely caught in the fold.

She found a camp site and then went to scout out something for supper. Coming across a grouse sitting on a low limb of a pine, she picked up a rock and threw it at him. He fell over dead. It was so easy to kill grouse that sometimes she thought it wasn't quite fair to do it. But she had to eat.

She put out her fire as soon as she had cooked the bird. She didn't want any visitors. That night she slept with the sling under her head.

chapter 19

About noon of the next day she approached the city of Butte. She had read a history of Butte once, and she was interested to see the city. It was built on hills. She looked around curiously as she rode up the street and decided it was a very ugly city, clinging to its steep hills as if it might fall off at any moment. Ringing the city were the mountains, barren and gashed open by copper mining operations.

She rode Hook up a steep hill. Remembering what her grandfather had said about asking directions at a filling station, she chose one that did not look too busy. Hook stepped on a hoselike thing that lay on the asphalt, and a bell rang. A boy came out of the station. He wore a blue shirt that said "Al" over the pocket, and a peaked cap on the back of his head. He gave her an amused grin. "Fill 'er up?"

She took out of her pocket the piece of paper on which her grandfather had written Uncle Arthur's name and address in his big bold handwriting. She handed it to the boy.

"Can you tell me how to find this place?"

He glanced at it. "You go to your second stop light and turn right. Go three blocks and then . . ." He stopped. He was looking at the paper more closely. "Arthur Bent?"

"Yes."

"I know Mr. Bent," he said. "He buys his gas here sometimes. He doesn't live there any more."

Laurie thought for a minute that she was just going to fall off Hook's back and lie down on the cement. It was too much. All that way and he didn't live here any more.

The boy was talking. "He lives out toward Anaconda," he said. "He bought him a ranch."

"How far?"

"Oh, five, six miles."

Laurie dismounted. She didn't feel up to another five or six miles. "Do you have a telephone?" she said.

"Sure. Inside. You can hitch your horse over there if you want." He pointed to the big metal handle on the door where the grease racks were.

Laurie hitched Hook and went inside. The place smelled of oil.

"Do you know his number?" the boy said.

She shook her head.

He took a greasy telephone book down off the shelf and thumbed through it. "Here it is." He handed it to her.

"How much will it cost?"

"A dime."

When she had fished a dime out of her wallet, she took down the receiver and dialled the number carefully. She heard the phone ring. It rang three times. He wasn't home. She was just about to hang up when a woman's voice said, "Hello?" It was the same voice she had heard before. "Hello?" it said again.

"Is Mr. Bent there?" Laurie said.

"Yes. Just a minute."

Her knees shook with relief. At last, at last. Then she heard Uncle Arthur's strong voice saying, "Yes?"

"Uncle Arthur," she said, "this is Laurie."

"Laurie! Where are you? Is everything all right?"

"Well, sort of all right," she said. "But I have to see you. I'm in Butte."

"In Butte! Where?"

She looked at the boy, who had been listening with unabashed interest. "Where is this?"

"Tell him the Gulf station where he trades."

"The Gulf station where you trade."

"I'll be right there," Uncle Arthur said.

"I've got my horse with me," she said.

"Your horse?" He sounded as if he couldn't believe it. Then he said, "Laurie, are you going to tell me you *rode* down here?"

"Yes," she said. "And I'm about played out."

"I'll be there in a few minutes. I'll bring the horse trailer. You just sit tight till I get there."

"All right." She hung up. She was there, and he was coming. She had to sit down. "Could I sit down for a minute?" she asked the boy.

"Sure. Help yourself." A car drove in and the bell rang. "I got to get that car." He sauntered out, whistling.

Laurie sat down in an old leather chair. She was not sure she would ever be able to get up.

She sat in the chair with her eyes closed. The boy came in and went out several times, and she heard the ring as cars drove in to be serviced. She was glad the boy was busy so she wouldn't have to talk.

"Laurie!"

Her eyes flew open. Uncle Arthur stood in the doorway. He looked even bigger than she had remembered him.

"Hi, Uncle Arthur." She got up stiffly.

"Are you all right?" he said.

"I'm fine. Just a little tired."

He took her arm. "I should think so. Is Pa all right?"

"Not entirely," she said. "That's why I came. He's going blind."

Uncle Arthur looked disturbed. "I was afraid something was wrong. I felt it in my bones. We were going up there this weekend."

She was too tired to ask who he meant by "we."

"You just make yourself comfortable in the pickup," he said. "I'll load your horse into the trailer."

She looked at the bright red horse trailer behind the new pickup.

"I'd better help," she said. "Hook has never been in one of those."

They went over to the horse, and Laurie led him to the

trailer. He balked at first but she talked to him soothingly and tugged at him gently and finally with a clatter of hoofs he scrambled up into it. He rolled his eyes wildly toward her.

"It's all right," she said. "You can ride for a change." She talked to him while Uncle Arthur attached the tailgate.

When Hook was calm, she climbed into the pickup.

"You're too tired to answer a lot of questions," Uncle Arthur said, "but just a couple: like, why in heaven's name didn't you take the bus? Or call me? And how did you hurt your arm?" He pointed to the bandage.

"Grandpa was afraid the police or somebody would pick me up and put me in an orphanage," she said. "I don't think now that they would have, but I didn't know. And I did call you, but you were out of town."

"That's right. I went to Wyoming to buy some cattle."

"My arm," she said, "—that happened when a rancher shot at me because he thought I was stealing his colt."

"A man like that ought to be jailed," Uncle Arthur said indignantly. He was pulling out of the gas station onto the street.

Laurie caught her breath. The man on the mule was coming down the street. His elbows flapped with the motion of the mule, like the wings of a bat. "That man . . ." she said.

Uncle Arthur glanced at him. "Oh, that's the local character," he said. "Old Hell-and-Damnation Hastings. He's peculiar, a little touched in the upper story. But he's harmless. Now," he said, turning his beaming face toward her, "let me tell you my news."

"What is it?" She looked back at the man on the mule.

He was bent over, and he looked old and somehow piti-
ful. For a second she had the odd feeling that she had
dreamed all that happened.

"I'm married!" Uncle Arthur looked at her with a
broad smile.

"Married!"

"Yes sir, what do you think of that? At my age! Pa
always said I was a born bachelor, and I thought so too
but here I am, forty-two years old, and married to the
prettiest little lady you ever laid eyes on. Her name is
Helen and you'll love her. We bought a ranch, and I've
really settled down."

"That's nice," she said. Uncle Arthur looked very
happy. She wondered what it would be like to have a
new aunt. She hoped the new aunt would like her.

She looked back once more as the pickup turned a
corner. The man on the mule looked small and far away.

chapter 20

"How bad is Pa?" Uncle Arthur asked.

Laurie told him the details.

"I'll leave right away," he said.

Laurie leaned back on the warm leather of the seat. "Gee, Uncle Arthur," she said, "I'm glad to see you."

He gave her a quick smile. "You've had too much of a load to carry by yourself. You've done a fine job. You just let me worry about things from here on out."

She felt so relieved, she almost wanted to cry. Uncle Arthur was so nice and solid.

He turned into a gravel road. "We're almost there," he said.

In a minute they drove up to a big white house.

"See?" he said. "We've got room for everybody. I bought the place with that in mind."

Beyond the house there was a barn and past the barn there was a big corral. She saw three horses in the corral. She hoped Hook would make friends with them. In the pasture in the distance she saw a herd of Black Angus.

"I'm raising beef cattle," Uncle Arthur said. "Got a fine herd. Pa can help me on the place. I really need him." He pulled up in front of the house.

The door of the house opened, and a woman stood there smiling. Laurie was almost afraid to look at her. What if the woman didn't like her?

"That's Helen," Uncle Arthur said happily. He jumped down from the pickup and came around to help Laurie down.

Laurie looked at Helen. She was a tall, slender, pretty woman, young-looking, with gray hair but it was pretty gray hair, cut short and curly. She had friendly brown eyes. She was wearing saddle pants and a white shirt.

"Helen," Uncle Arthur said. . . .

But before he could finish, Helen came toward Laurie with her hands outstretched.

"This is Laurie," she said. She took both Laurie's hands in a warm squeeze. "I'm so glad you're here. I've heard so much about you."

"I hadn't heard about you at all," Laurie said, "until the last few minutes." Then she stopped, afraid that she had said the wrong thing.

But Helen laughed. "Come on in the house," she said. "You must be dead tired."

"My horse . . ." Laurie began.

"I'll take care of him," Uncle Arthur said. "I'll be

right with you." And as Laurie hesitated, looking at Hook, he said, "We'll get along all right. He looks like a smart horse."

Helen took Laurie into the house. It was cool and pretty, with big high-ceilinged rooms. "Would you like to go up to your room first?"

"My room?"

"Yes. We've been fixing up rooms for you and your grandfather. Arthur was worried about you. In fact we were going to come up this weekend to see if we could get you to move down here with us."

Laurie had never imagined living anywhere except at the ghost town. The idea dismayed her, though not so much as it once would have, she knew.

Her room was pretty. "Any time you want to redecorate it or do anything to it, you just go ahead and do it," Helen said. "It's yours." She sat down on the edge of the bed and smiled at Laurie. Her eyes were warm. "I think we're going to be good friends."

"I think so, too," Laurie said.

"Arthur has talked about you so much. He's worried about you, but he wasn't in a position to do much. We've talked about your schooling. You ought to be in a regular school."

"Well, I take my correspondence stuff," Laurie said. She didn't want Aunt Helen to think that Grandfather hadn't taken care of things.

"You should be in a real school, though."

"That's what Grandfather says, too, so I guess soon I will be."

"Arthur says you're awfully smart." She got up. "The bathroom is in there. You take a nap or whatever you feel like. Are you hungry?"

"No, thank you." Laurie was too excited to be hungry.

"I'll call you later then."

Laurie took a long bath, so long she almost fell asleep in the tub. When she came back to the bedroom, there was a glass of milk and some cookies on the table. She felt taken care of, and it was nice. But she would be awfully glad to see Grandfather. Now that she had accomplished the trip, she began to be homesick.

She lay down on the bed. When she woke up, Helen was standing beside her.

"Feel like something to eat now?" she said.

"Yes." Laurie sat up.

"Arthur has already left to get your grandfather. They should be back tomorrow."

"Tomorrow!" Laurie thought of all the days it had taken her.

"Come down when you're ready."

While she was eating, Laurie said, "Will Grandfather have to go to a hospital?"

"Probably," Helen said. "Arthur thinks he has cataracts. He says he's seen it coming on. But he wouldn't have to be in the hospital long."

"He's scared of hospitals," Laurie said. "He's afraid they'll never let him out."

"Hospitals nowadays are so crowded, they can't wait to let you out."

"Will it hurt him?"

"No. We have a fine eye doctor here who will take care of everything." She cleared the plates away and brought Laurie a big strawberry shortcake. "Did you have adventures on your trip?"

"Yes," Laurie said, "quite a few."

"When you're rested, maybe you'll tell us about them." Helen leaned her chin on her hand, looking at Laurie. "That was quite a valiant thing you did."

"I don't know," Laurie said. "It had to be done."

"Arthur asked me to take you to our doctor to make sure your arm is coming along all right. I made an appointment for late this afternoon."

"Oh, all right," Laurie said. That would take care of her promise to Dr. Ashe.

Helen's doctor was rather an old man but he was very nice. He examined Laurie's arm carefully. "Somebody did a good job on this," he said. "Who took care of you?"

"Dr. Ashe."

He nodded. "I know Ashe. He's a good man." He put a Band-Aid over the wound. "It's healed up nicely. You may have a little scar as a souvenir."

When they left the doctor's office, Helen asked her if there was anything she would like to do.

"I wish I could get my hair cut," Laurie said.

The beauty parlor was astonishing. She realized now that was what she had seen in Missoula. Women were sitting in chairs with their hair done up in the most amazing contraptions. Some of them sat under big silver domes that roared. Laurie felt some alarm. But the girl who took her in charge just cut her hair without any nonsense. She was pleased with the results. She had never had it cut that way before. She looked older. There's a new me getting born, she thought, and it gave her a funny feeling.

When they got home she visited Hook. She took him

some sugar and rode him bareback around the pasture. Then she came back to the house, feeling restless. She couldn't get used to not being on the move. Helen had gone to get in some groceries so Laurie wandered all over the house. It was big, with four bedrooms and two bathrooms. She hadn't realized that people lived in such big houses. She thought it would make her feel kind of lost. It was a comfortable house though, and it had two television sets but not many books. This could be her house.

She went outside and sat on the steps. It made her uneasy to be inside too much. She tried to think about whether she would like to live there, but all she could feel was a longing for Grandfather and the cabin.

chapter 21

When Laurie heard the pickup drive in late the next morning, she ran out. "Grandpa!" She opened his door and helped him out. He moved stiffly.

"Hello, Laurie," he said. He gave her a quick hug. "Arthur says you made out all right."

"I had some high old adventures."

"Bet you did. I'll be anxious to hear about them."

She could tell he was uneasy and worried.

Helen came out and took his hand. "Welcome, Mr. Bent. I'm Helen."

"Glad to meet you," he said formally. "I never figured on having a daughter-in-law."

"Wait till you get your eyes fixed, Pa," Uncle Arthur

said. "You'll see what a beauty she is."

"You always did like the best," his father said.

Helen took his arm and led him toward the house.

When he was sitting in an easy chair in the living room, he said to Laurie, "Arthur's got some ideas about the mine."

"I've had a hunch for a long time that there's silver in that mine," Uncle Arthur said.

"I know good and well there is."

"Well, the price of silver is up. What I figure we can do is hire some guy with power equipment, a bulldozer and all that, and let him go at it."

"Bulldozer?" Grandfather sat stiffly on the edge of his chair as if he didn't quite trust the new room yet.

"That's the way to do it now. Faster and easier and a whole lot more efficient. You can clean up. But you don't need to do it yourself, you see; you don't even need to be there."

"Be there?" his father said. "I'd have to be there. That's my place."

"We hoped that you and Laurie would live with us now," Helen said. "We have lots of room."

Laurie watched her grandfather anxiously. He didn't say anything for a minute. Then he said, "That's mighty nice of you, but I'm no hand for living off other folks."

"Pa," Uncle Arthur said, "we're your family."

"I know that," his father said. "And I am grateful you want us. But I'm an independent old cuss, Arthur, always was. Laurie, now, that's a different matter, I guess." He sighed heavily and folded his hands over the top of his cane.

Laurie didn't want the conversation to take this turn.

"How much would it cost, that bulldozer thing, Uncle Arthur?" she asked.

"Not a whole lot. I could lend you what you need to get started."

"I'm glad it's not a whole lot," his father said drily. "I got about ten dollars to my name, free and clear."

"And three gold nuggets," Laurie said.

"I'll back you," Uncle Arthur said again. "You can sell me a share in the mine if you want to."

"I got to see before I can do anything. Can't handle anything when I can't see my hand before my face."

"You've got an appointment with Dr. Mann in the morning," Helen said. "He's a fine man, Mr. Bent."

"I ain't going to any hospital," he said quickly.

"Pa," Uncle Arthur said quietly, "you might have to go for a few days. It won't kill you."

"They never let you out of there alive."

"Look," Uncle Arthur said, "trust me. I'm not going to let anybody do anything you don't want. You know that."

"You always were a good boy," his father said.

"I'm still a good boy, so quit worrying."

The next morning Dr. Mann diagnosed Peter Bent's problem as cataracts. Later Laurie and her grandfather sat on the porch together.

"I guess I got to go through with it," he said. "But I don't want to do it. I don't want to go into any infernal hospital."

"Aunt Helen says they're so crowded now, they never keep anybody any longer than they have to," Laurie said. Her heart ached for him. "We wouldn't let them keep you even if they wanted to. Uncle Arthur and I

174

wouldn't let them."

He nodded. "The doctor gave his word. So did Arthur." He leaned his head back. "Well, what's got to be has got to be, I guess."

"Think how nice it will be when your eyes are all right again."

It was a long time before he answered. "I'm an old man, Laurie, an old man."

"You're not!" she said. "You aren't old at all. As soon as you can see again, you'll beat me fishing."

He smiled sadly. "We'll see. We'll see."

chapter 22

Uncle Arthur and Aunt Helen kept assuring her that the operation had been completely successful, but Laurie was very frightened. When they took her to see her grandfather, she understood his feeling about hospitals. People were nice enough, but there were all those rooms with sick people in them, and everybody in white. She heard somebody moan, and it scared her half to death but it wasn't Grandfather.

He was lying very still in a high bed with a bandage over his eyes. She thought he must be going to die.

"Come along in, dear," a nurse said to her. "Mr. Bent is awake."

Aunt Helen and Uncle Arthur let her go ahead of

them. Cautiously she went up to the bed. "Grandfather?"
Her voice sounded high and squeaky.

He turned his head. "That you, Laurie?"

"Yes."

"Well, they tell me I'm going to see again." His voice
sounded unexpectedly strong.

She grabbed his hand and squeezed it in relief. "Oh,
good!"

Uncle Arthur laughed. "What did I tell you?"

"Doctor says it'll be six weeks or more before I can go
back to the cabin. I'll have to get some glasses, he tells
me. I never thought I'd have to wear glasses."

"Millions of people wear glasses," Uncle Arthur said.

"It doesn't kill them."

"Guess not," his father said. "I've been lying here thinking about Gertrude."

"Who is Gertrude?" Aunt Helen said.

"Pa's cow," Uncle Arthur said. "We had to sell her."

"I was wondering if I could buy her back. I miss Gertrude."

"Well, if you can't get Gertrude, you can get another cow. A cow's a cow," Uncle Arthur said.

"That's where you're wrong," his father said. "You ought to know better than that, Arthur."

Arthur laughed. "O.K., Pa."

"What am I going to do, sitting around your place for six weeks or so? I'm no hand for sitting around."

"Don't worry, I'll put you to work," Uncle Arthur said. "There's plenty of work."

When he had been out of the hospital for about a week, he said to Arthur, "We got to get going on plans for the mine."

"I'll get in touch with some people tomorrow," Arthur said. "I know just the right bunch."

"Are they honest?"

"As the day is long."

"That mine's going to make us all rich, you know."

"Well, it may not do quite that, but I think it will bring in some money all right."

Laurie thought about the mine. It would be different at Hawkins Dry Diggins, with strangers working there. She was not sure she would like it. But of course making the mine pay off had been her grandfather's dream for years. She sighed. It was bewildering, the way things changed.

chapter 23

A week or so before her grandfather was finally ready to go back home, Laurie was invited to have lunch in town with Aunt Helen. She prepared for it carefully, putting on one of her new dresses and combing and combing her hair to get the cowlick to lie down.

"You look like a little princess," Uncle Arthur said, when she came downstairs.

"Looks like her grandma," her grandfather said.

It was a new experience to have her appearance remarked upon, and it made her both pleased and self-conscious. On the whole she decided she liked it.

Aunt Helen took her to the Finlen Hotel for lunch. It was a little frightening at first, and Laurie kept watching

Aunt Helen to make sure she did the right thing. She knew her table manners were all right because Grandfather had seen to that, but she was not used to the big menu, the waiter standing at her elbow, and all the rest of it.

Aunt Helen said, "What would you like, dear?" and she just didn't know.

"I think I'll have the crab salad," Aunt Helen said to the waiter, "and iced coffee."

"What kind of dressing?" the waiter said, and Laurie felt pleased that she knew what he was talking about.

"Thousand Island." She smiled reassuringly at Laurie.

"I'll have that too," Laurie said quickly. "Only milk instead of coffee."

The waiter went away, and Laurie relaxed. It hadn't been so bad.

It was a very good lunch, and they had blueberry cobbler for dessert. After the waiter had brought Aunt Helen a second glass of iced coffee, Aunt Helen leaned back and said, "I wanted to talk to you alone, Laurie."

Oh dear, Laurie thought, what now? She felt herself stiffening for whatever might come.

"Your grandfather is almost ready to go home." Aunt Helen paused, as if she were not quite sure how to say what she wanted to say. "Your uncle and I have been talking a good deal about you."

"Me?"

"Yes." Again she paused. "Laurie, we would love to have you stay on with us, live with us, if you'd like to." She said it quickly, and Laurie realized that Aunt Helen felt nervous, too.

"That's awfully nice of you." It *was* nice. It was so

nice, that for a second she thought she was going to cry. "But I couldn't let Grandfather go home alone. He's going to need me."

Aunt Helen stirred her coffee slowly. "We thought you would say that. And it's understandable. You two are very close."

"He might get sick or something. Besides, it's . . . it's my home too. I love it there." She thought again, as she had thought so often lately, of riding Hook free through that wild country. Nothing could take the place of that. Wading in an ice-cold mountain stream, picking wild flowers in the meadow, just looking and looking at the mountains and the way the light turned them all different colors from gold to purple to green . . .

"There will be other people there, of course, at least while they're working on the mine, so he wouldn't be alone."

But they wouldn't go fishing with him and get crowned queen of the fish, and they wouldn't catch him a choice rabbit, or cook corn dodgers for him, or listen to his stories about the old days. And yet she knew it was going to be different. She had changed. She had learned to enjoy things like bathtubs and fancy meals and symphonies and access to books she hadn't already read. . . . She had learned to pay attention to people.

"We would love to have you stay here," Aunt Helen said, a little wistfully. "But even if you decide not to, we want to adopt you legally, if you have no objection."

"Adopt me?" She had never thought of such a thing. "Wouldn't I belong to Grandfather any more?"

"Of course you would. Nothing could change that. But if you were our adopted child, we could do more, protect you better . . ."

"Keep me out of the orphanage?"

"I think you've outgrown the orphanage threat, but we could send you to college, look after you—and this would be your home, too, when you needed it." She shook her head. "I'm not putting it very well. Of course we could do all those things without adopting you. I guess it's just that we would love to have you for our daughter."

Impulsively Laurie reached out and touched Aunt Helen's hand. "You're very good to me."

"We love you."

Laurie traced a design on the white linen tablecloth with the handle of her spoon. "I love you, too, both of you." She felt terribly torn. Here were two worlds and she loved them both, but she had to choose.

Aunt Helen reached for the check and pushed back her chair. "You think about it, dear. Nobody is going to pressure you."

chapter 24

A few days before it was time for Grandfather to go home, he and Laurie sat on the porch after dinner, rocking comfortably. Her grandfather still could not see very distinctly, but the doctor said he was coming along fine.

"Arthur's got a nice place here," he said.

"Yes." She looked out across the corrals and pasture. She could see Hook grazing with some of Uncle Arthur's horses. In the farthest meadow a man was haying. Everything was so well taken care of.

"They're real anxious to have you stay with them. Go to school here and all."

Laurie had had time to think about it, and she knew what she had to do. "I'm going home with you."

He searched her face. "You'd have a lot of advantages here that I can't give you."

"You've given me advantages nobody else could."

"Arthur says they'd like to adopt you. I think it's a good idea."

"I do, too," she said. "I'd like to have kind of like parents. But I'm going to live with you." Maybe she could get one of those phonographs that played on batteries or whatever it was. And she could save money for records and books. She'd talk to Uncle Arthur about that fish-smoking idea.

"Well, one thing," he said, "if you come back with me, you're going to a regular school. You could ride Hook into town."

"All right."

"I told Arthur, if you come home with me, you'd come down here for your vacations. What do you think of that?"

"That would be fine."

"They'll see that you go to a good college when the time comes. Then you can be a teacher, like your grandmother and your daddy."

Laurie had been thinking about that. She thought she might like to be a teacher. But at least she didn't have to decide *that* right now. "Maybe I can pay my own way to college, when the Saturday Mine gets working."

He chuckled. "You and me, we're an independent pair of cusses." He pulled his old pipe out of his pocket and filled it carefully, tamping it down with his thumb. "One thing we got to keep in mind though—when folks love you, it gives 'em pleasure to do for you. I guess it's kind of selfish to be too doggoned independent."

Laurie looked out over the fields. A dense cloud of blackbirds appeared, flying over the field, and as if on signal they dropped to the ground. In a few minutes they rose again, some of them wheeling away, some of them settling back on the telephone line so close together they almost seemed to touch.

"There's a flock of blackbirds," Laurie said.

"They make a pretty sight."

Laurie watched the one on the end, and a line of the Sylvia Plath poem came into her mind. "I only know that a rook Ordering its feathers can so shine As to seize my senses . . ." Someday soon she'd have to write Miss Emily. She had a feeling Miss Emily would approve of her going back to the mine, just as long as she didn't shut out the good in the world again.

A crow flew down toward the wire and the birds rose again in a fluttering black mass and flew away. The crow balanced awkwardly on the wire, flapping his wings to keep from falling.

"Do you believe in the devil?" Laurie asked.

"Never took much stock in him."

"Some people could almost be the devil, the wicked way they act."

"That's sure enough so. Those are the ones to look out for."

She took her peacock feather out of her pocket and smoothed it out. "And yet there's some awfully good people. I guess you have to sort it out as you go along."

"Just watch out for those institutions." Her grandfather sounded drowsy. After a few minutes he said, "Alec Begg came to see me."

"He's a nice man."

"None better. He told me you kicked some young feller in the shins."

She looked at him anxiously to see if he disapproved. "He hit Hook."

Her grandfather smiled. "I guess you made your point all right. But there's better ways of handling these things. A young lady don't go around kicking folks in the shins."

"I'm not a young lady."

"Yes, you are, and we've got to make you a good one. That's where Helen and Arthur can help a lot. You got to learn how to wear dresses and all that."

"I don't feel comfortable in a dress."

"You got to look and act like a lady."

Laurie thought about it. "I don't know if I'll ever make it."

"You'll make it all right. You're your grandmother's spitting image. And your mother was a lady. You'll make a fine woman." He paused in his rocking. "You real sure you want to go home with me?"

"I'm sure."

Her grandfather was quiet for so long that she thought he had fallen asleep. But then he began to sing softly.

> It takes a worried man
> To sing a worried song . . .

Laurie joined in with him and their voices rose on the evening air.